# THE LEGACY OF GLORIA RUSSELL

SHERI L. GILBERT

ALFRED A. KNOPF
NEW YORK

Many thanks to my fabulous agent and crit partners. This story wouldn't be what it is without you, gals. In addition, a huge measure of appreciation to my editor, Michelle, who helped me whittle the story straight to its very heart.

THIS IS A BORZOI BOOK PUBLISHED BY ALFRED A. KNOPF
Copyright © 2004 by Sheri L. Gilbert.
Jacket illustration and spot art copyright © 2004 by Wendy Schultz Wubbels.
All rights reserved under International and Pan-American Copyright Conventions.
Published in the United States by Alfred A. Knopf, an imprint of Random House
Children's Books, a division of Random House, Inc., New York, and simultaneously in
Canada by Random House of Canada Limited, Toronto.
Distributed by Random House, Inc., New York.

KNOPF, BORZOI BOOKS, and the colophon are registered trademarks of Random House, Inc.

www.randomhouse.com/kids

*Library of Congress Cataloging-in-Publication Data*
Gilbert, Sheri L.
The legacy of Gloria Russell / Sheri L. Gilbert. — 1st ed.
    p. cm.
SUMMARY: Twelve-year-old Billy James tries to come to terms with the sudden death of
his best friend and learns about himself, his own family history, and life in his small
hometown in the Ozark mountains.
ISBN 0-375-82823-0 (trade) — ISBN 0-375-92823-5 (lib. bdg.)
[1. Death—Fiction. 2. Family life—Missouri—Fiction. 3. Mountain life—Missouri—
Fiction. 4. Missouri—Fiction.] I. Title.
PZ7.G3793Le 2004
[Fic]—dc22    2003017423

Printed in the United States of America
April 2004
10 9 8 7 6 5 4 3 2 1
First Edition

TO KRIS AND LANCE, THE TWO MOST BALANCED MINDS ON THE PLANET. AND MOM AND DAD, WHO LET ME KEEP MY HEAD IN THE CLOUDS.

—S.L.G.

# CHAPTER 1

From the moment she touched Satan, Gloria Russell was never the same. Only a week later, she started wearing so much black she all but melted into midnight. She'd even dyed her sandy hair coal-black, and slathered on purple lipstick, which made her look like she'd stuck her face into Gram's famous Standby Plum Jam and gone right to town, forgetting to wipe her mouth. If it wasn't for her moon-pale face, she might've disappeared entirely after dark.

Which would've been fine with some. But not with me. Not having my best friend around anymore felt like someone had chopped off my right arm; she haunted me like a ghost limb. I'd turn and swear Gloria was still beside me, her skinny legs swinging over the water-tower deck, her wicked grin lighting up the night.

Sweat popped out on my forehead and I wiped at it with my T-shirt. Satan might not have directly *caused* Gloria's death, but that February touch started it all, sure as shootin'.

I figured there had to be *some* rational reason we'd been warned since we were old enough to figure: Stay clear of Satan. Maybe a polite hello (we weren't rude folk), but never, ever a touch.

Gloria said it never made a lick of sense why the old-timers hated the hermit. His name alone shouldn't have mattered. It was a foreign name, Czechoslovakian or something. Gloria and I came to the conclusion that Satan had a criminal record they didn't want us kids to know about. The old-timers were always saying, "Leave him be and mind your own business."

Which wasn't hard to do, since Satan kept to himself, only coming into town when he needed to stock up before the winter gales, or after the black sod finished drinking in the patchy March snow. Him showing up in mid-February should've alerted me to the fact that things were about to jump track, but all I could think on was why he tried to hide himself behind those wide-brimmed hats and long trench coats.

"Best not to think about him at all, Billy James," Mama had said when I pondered that question aloud. "You mind your own, that's all. Mind your own."

And I did, mostly.

But not Gloria.

She had to know everything about everything. "Who busted up your lip, Billy?" Or, "Why don't they yank that dogwood tree that's cracking the concrete downtown, Billy?" Or sometimes, if I didn't give her an answer that doused her catlike curiosity, she'd move on to a higher-up: "Mrs. Wilkins, where's Billy's daddy?"

That was four years ago, the last day Mama had invited Gloria Russell over after school. "Eight-year-old girls got no cause to be asking questions like that!"

Mama had said in one of her huffs, slamming plates and snapping her towel like she was trying to rip a seam in the air.

But we kept hanging out thick as thieves, as Gram said, and just as ornery. But not near as ornery as my older brother, Ray. To Ray I was Gnat. That's what he'd called me since birth, which was what everyone else starting calling me soon after. Except Mama. It was Billy James with her, both first and middle as if they were one, just like Ray was Raymond Clay, no matter that he's eighteen now and out on his own. I knew it couldn't be easy for Ray, especially with what he makes at the mill, but having him out of the house was like coming up from the bottom of a cold lake and breathing fresh air.

Gloria never tolerated any of Ray's guff. She'd plant her hands on her hips and mouth off something fierce, until Ray started for her, then she'd beat feet to whatever safe spot we'd arranged on ahead of time. We'd laugh until our sides near split at the firecracker look on Ray's face.

Since school started in September, things had been normal—almost perfect, actually, until February rolled around and Satan showed up in town.

Seemed like maybe the old-timers were right. Touching Josef Satan *was* a surefire prescription for disaster. Funny how Gloria swore differently. It's not like I didn't *want* to believe her. I wished I could tell her that, not that it matters now. No way she could hear me, buried under so much dirt like she is.

Gram said Gloria can. She says, "There's listening

with your body ears and listening with your spirit ears." According to Gram, Gloria's spirit ears are on all the time now, and she can hear what I'm trying to say without me saying it aloud. I might've believed that, but there's one thing I could never hold as true, and that's that there's a God with His hand in man's business.

No way that could be true, because if it were, Gloria Russell would be on the water tower with me enjoying the fine May evening. She'd be singing one of those melancholy hymns she learned in youth choir till I threatened to push her over the edge if she didn't shut her mouth. She'd laugh, of course, because Gloria didn't take orders from anyone.

I wondered if there would ever be a time when remembering Gloria (which I did every other minute) didn't feel like I was dying a little bit myself.

*Okay, Billy, think of something else for a change.* I flicked on my flashlight and opened my favorite comic, but my thoughts kept drifting back to Gloria's box. The one she made me take the night before she passed on three weeks ago.

Pulling the box into my lap, I ran my hands over its rough, grainy exterior. Gloria had covered it with bits of straw, dirt, and pebbles. The glue was already starting to wear, and great gobs of gunk were peeling off.

I worked a finger under the biggest flap and touched the cool blue metal beneath.

*You gotta make the stuff you treasure the most unappealing thing around, Billy. It needs to be unappealing and invisible all in the same breath. Understand?*

Unappealing and invisible. Funny thing was, Gloria

was the most visible person I ever knew. Even before she dyed her hair and all that stuff, she stood out. Not on the outside, but on the inside. On the outside she looked pretty much like everyone else. Medium height, slightly wavy wheat-colored hair, brown eyes, and average clothes. Her nose was turned up a bit, and she had what Mama called a stubborn chin, tense, like she was gearing up to let you know what she thought. Sorta like Mama, come to think of it.

But the inside was where Gloria was different. Once she opened her mouth, you knew she wasn't at all ordinary or plain. She had ideas that would blow you out of the water just to think of 'em.

"Maybe there was a secret blood-drinking cult in the hills, and that's what drove everyone down to the valley."

Or . . .

"I've come to the conclusion that this town is a government experiment run by the CIA."

Or . . .

"You think your Gram still makes moonshine in those hills behind her house, Billy?"

Crazy stuff.

It's no wonder people began to think her a couple of cards shy of a full deck when her questions and stories didn't fade into the background along with our childhood. The kicker was, I had listened to her long enough to almost believe some of the stuff she said.

Forcing my head back to the here and now, I checked my watch and figured I'd better head back. Ray'd be gone for sure, and Mama would be back from the diner and getting worried. I tucked Gloria's box under my arm and headed for the ladder. I'd glue the flaps down at home.

With the moon barely a sliver, I was careful to climb down with a mind to where I put my "battleship" feet. Aircraft carriers, that was what Mama called them: "Billy James, if your feet grow any bigger, I swear we're gonna have to trim back toes so you don't put me in the poorhouse!"

It was a terrible shame that the rest of my body hadn't caught up to my feet. Four-feet-nine, rough-cut dusty brown hair, and thin as stretched taffy, I was not an impressive seventh grader. I could run respectably well (learned that out of necessity), but I couldn't hit, kick, or catch a fly ball to save my life. Not that I didn't try. What else was there to do in Kelseyville if you weren't into sports?

Not much.

It was baseball and softball at Clemmens Field all day Sunday, and football games on Friday nights. My friend Hog had taken a real shine to sports since fall rolled around last year. Hardly saw him at all anymore.

"Get involved, Billy James," Mama said. "Team sports teach cooperation."

I snorted at the memory. Oh, yeah, look what baseball did for Raymond Clay. Taught him how to be top dog in a pack of porch hounds. Big help.

But as I made my way past Culloden Crick toward our farm, it got me to thinking, what am I good at?

Well, I can fix things.

Pretty ironic how my fingers can twist, tighten, and

repair, yet refuse to hold on to a football or catch a pop fly. Gram says I've a true knack for knowing what's wrong with something, before feeling my way around the fix. That's what she calls it, all creepy like, "the fix." As if it's some type of magical power. I don't hold with that. I just seem to be able to understand the inner operations of things, and see my way to putting them back in working order, that's all.

Deep, rich scents filled my nose and slowed my thoughts. Mrs. O'Dell's lilacs were blooming early from all the rain. I sneezed, the sweet aroma going straight to my head.

"Who—who's there? You stay away, hear me? Stay away!"

It was a boy's voice, young and panicky. But not one I recognized, which was odd. In a town of nine hundred, you pretty much knew everyone inside and out, whether you wanted to or not.

"I'm not gonna hurt you, whoever you are." I crouched and peered into the shadows. A loud stumble and crack told me he was retreating through the scrub and heading into the soybean fields.

I checked my watch again. It was almost ten o'clock. Way too late for a little kid to be out wandering the woods and fields. Too late for a twelve-year-old like me, too. If I didn't get home soon, Mama'd not only be worried sick, but more dangerous than an underfed sow.

"Dang it," I whispered, then trotted after the retreating crunches.

# CHAPTER 2

The boy left a ragged trail, crashing through as if the devil himself were hot on his heels. No use calling out, it'd just scare him more, so I saved my breath and followed close. My feet thumped into the fertile soil, stirring up earthy scents and pollen to tickle my nose.

The sneezes started coming then, one right after the other. With my eyes watering and a hand to my dripping nose, I stumbled practically right on top of his hunched back, bent over like he was, face first in the irrigation ditch. Lucky for him the ditch wasn't full, just mucky with the last dregs of river water meant for the soybean crop.

I pulled the boy up while he sputtered, "Lemmego! Lemmego!"

He had gone plumb wild, but since I was holding him by his shirt collar, there wasn't anything for his fists to connect with but air.

"I'm not gonna hurt you. Stop all that kicking and hush up before we have old man Westerfield after us with his shotgun."

His mud-encrusted eyes went wide, whites glowing

in the gloom. He calmed right down, but there was an angry set to his mouth.

The black mud released his tennis shoes with a gloopy *pop* as I pulled him from the ditch. "I'm gonna let go, but you stay put, hear?" I tried to use Mama's best authoritative tone. It was passable good, but it wasn't going to carry the same weight, so I stayed in tight as I released his collar.

He pushed a hank of muddy hair out of his eyes, then fixed me with a hunted stare, as if he had been caught in some leg trap and was getting set to gnaw off his foot.

"Let's have some introductions." I held out my hand. "My name's Billy James Wilkins."

His face screwed up like he'd chomped on a bitter caterpillar. "You can't make me stay, Billy whoever-you-are. I won't stay here with her, I won't! I'm going back to Palm Springs soon as I find the airport! Got it?"

What with spit flying and fists at his sides, the boy meant business. As I looked him over, I realized he might be closer to eight than seven. He was mighty short, but definitely well fed. His cheeks were round and rosy and his bare arms were thick above the elbow where they met his brick-red polo shirt.

"Well, all I know is being out in the woods at night's no place for a kid," I said. "Especially one that doesn't live here in town."

Didn't take a rocket scientist to figure that part out. The kid screamed city more than Aunt Gessie May when she graced us country bumpkins with her presence.

"Are you lost or something?" I asked.

His virulent (one of Gloria's favorite words) look

faltered for a second, then he straightened, starchlike. "I am *not* lost. I'm very good at directions. My dad says so."

"Okay, then, where were you headed?" I asked, knowing full well he hadn't a clue where he was.

His lower lip jutted out. "I won't tell you! Not if you torture me with a thousand needles, you dirty old hillbilly!"

I laughed. *Old hillbilly?*

Sure, Kelseyville wasn't a big-city type of place, and yeah, we were more country than a lot of other places, but it wasn't like I was wearing ripped overalls and sole-flapping shoes (oh, wait a minute, my shoes were pretty ragged, come to think of it) and chewing on a grass stem (I'd thrown that away before I climbed down from the tower).

Well, I certainly wasn't *old*.

He stared back openmouthed. He hadn't expected me to laugh. I looked at him with what I hoped was a firm stare. "Now, you ought not to be callin' names. Some might take offense." I wasn't offended. He was worked up, and scared.

*Where did he say he was from?* Palm Springs? Movie stars and fancy resorts. Trendy coffee houses on every corner. The Ozarks must feel like the other side of the world to him. "Look, you might *want* to be on your way to Palm Springs, but we don't have an airport here, and the train station won't let a seven-year-old—"

"I'm eight!" He stood straight as can be, baby pudge falling over the lip of his jeans like a roll of Mama's sweet dough.

I didn't laugh this time. "All right. They won't let an *eight*-year-old board this time of night without an adult."

His face was dang near hanging on the ground, and his eyes were fast-filling shiny pools. He'd had his heart set on leaving tonight, come hell or high water.

He turned away, and I put a hand on his shoulder, only to have him knock my arm away.

"Then I'll camp out here until morning. I'll . . ."—he shuffled his feet and took deep breaths—". . . find a good spot and wait till the sun comes up. No big deal!" he finished with a shout, as if challenging me to find a flaw in his reasoning.

I could've. There were plenty of flaws, but I wasn't going to be the one to tell him that. He was being driven by something *soul deep,* as Gram called it. Soul-deep issues can't be excised by the power of a word, she said. Even a string of 'em.

Question was, what to do with him? I couldn't bring him home with me. It wasn't that Mama wouldn't take him in. She would without a word otherwise, but his presence alone wouldn't stop her from letting me have it for being out so late. The boy was uptight, and hearing a tongue-lashing by my mama wouldn't make him feel any better. He'd probably run off all over again.

A picture of Ray and his posse came to mind. It might not be someone like me that found him next time.

That settled it.

"Listen up, Palm Springs. You're gonna stay with my Gram tonight."

He started sputtering, but I clapped my hands together like a gunshot. "No choice. Understand?" It wasn't a good thing to split his intent in two, but he couldn't be left on his own, either. Best to simply pull rank.

I waited for him to nod, which he never did; just glowered at me with those big brown eyes. That counted for adequate understanding, if not agreement.

"Let's go." I picked up Gloria's box, then grabbed the boy's shoulder and steered him in the right direction. He went stiffly, his short legs dragging through the scrub.

Once back on the path, I started for the deeper woods north of the crick. The closer we got to the trees, the slower he walked. I knew what he was thinking. I would've thought the same, probably.

I stopped. "Look, I'm not leading you into the woods to do you in. My Gram lives about half a mile away, behind that stand of trees and up the hill. She's the only person left on Cane's Hill. Everyone moved to the valley a long time ago, where they could farm and make a living. There are only a few hard-bitten folk stayed in the hills, and my Gram's one of them, and her Gram before that."

And Satan. But I wasn't about to mention the old hermit.

We started walking again. His feet didn't drag so much, but his body was as straight as new-cut lumber. He would never make it up Gram's hill that rigid. The mountain would leach off his energy right quick and then some.

Flexing my arms, I sighed. It was only a matter of time before they'd be needed for some heavy work.

# CHAPTER 3

oy? What you got there?"

I trudged the final few yards, my arms on fire from the load they'd borne for the last quarter mile—uphill.

Palm Springs had agreed to go piggyback after much smooth talking on my part and threats on his if he were dropped. I'd left Gloria's box in a bush halfway up Gram's mountain, which was about when the boy had fallen asleep. I eased him around front with only a murmur and wet snort for my troubles.

"Got a package for you, Gram," I said, not surprised to find her on the front stoop waiting for me.

"Hmph," she said, holding the screen door open.

The repairs I had made to her front steps still looked good. Hardly squeaked at all as I hefted my burden up the stairs, across the porch, and into the cabin. It was warm inside, a low fire burning behind the grate, filling the room with a strong tang of hickory and pine.

Gram motioned to her sewing room and I went inside, laying the boy on the trundle bed. He stirred a tiny bit, his face pinched even in sleep, but he didn't wake.

I lowered the curtain that made up the only door in Gram's two-room cabin and joined her by the fire, sitting across from her in a hardbacked chair.

"You're out late, Billy James," she said.

I nodded.

"Your mama's gonna be fit to be tied when you get back."

"Yep."

Her sharp black eyes drilled right through me. "You'd better get on."

"Yeah, guess I'd better." My lips cracked, the tinny taste of fresh scab filling my mouth. Once outside, I turned. "He's eight. And he's good at directions. His daddy says so."

Gram nodded without looking up.

I made my way down the hill to retrieve Gloria's box and head home.

Despite Mama's harsh words embedded in my skin like sharp stones, I slept deep, then woke to the spicy aroma of cinnamon and honey starter rolls and strong-brewed coffee. I winced while pulling on my work boots, my arms tight as Jammin' Cat's guitar strings.

I wondered if Cat would be at Greystokes tonight, or if his sweetheart's arrival would put a stop to it. There was nothing better than listening to Jammin' Cat pick away, which I did on the nights Mama delivered her pies, sweet rolls, and breads to Greystokes, the only roadside diner and nightclub for forty miles around. She rolled out the next day's biscuits and dinner rolls, so there was plenty of time to listen to Cat play.

Gloria's mama used to take her there on Friday and Saturday nights. Everyone liked to go on the nights that Cat played. A clear memory scrolled through my mind. Gloria, sitting next to Cat, her hands pounding out a rhythm on her skinny legs as Cat picked, his eyes closed, his lips quirked in a half smile.

Cat's music had been somber since Gloria's passing. Hearing it was like finding out for the first time all over again. But he was playing his feelings, and I could relate to that, even if listening just about killed me.

"Well, it's about time!" Mama griped as I walked into the kitchen. "You think I got nothing better to do than keep this breakfast warm for a boy who don't know when to get his scrawny butt home at night?"

If it had been Ray, she wouldn't have complained. But I wasn't about to tell her that. Besides, the rolls were fresh, not ones she'd kept on the back burner. She wiped the stove with serious muscle power, the sleeves of her "I Saw Barbara Mandrell in Branson!" T-shirt stretched tight over well-formed biceps. I couldn't help but peek at my own lanky arms. Daddy must've been one skinny dude, with all his stick-thin genes landing in my pool.

"These are heaven, Mama," I said around a mouthful. And they were. Everyone agreed that Mama's sweet rolls were the best of the best. Their eye-rolling sweetness made up for her chronic sourness in most everyone's eyes.

"Hmph," she muttered as she continued to clean, pausing every now and then to catch her breath. Mama and Gram had that single-syllable, message-packed expression down. When Sarah Wilkins "hmphed" at you, you knew she had decided you were all right for the time being.

"Mama, I need to go out to Gram's after chores. Her roof's leakin' again." Which wasn't exactly true. It had never stopped leaking, even after Ray had finally gone up last summer and supposedly patched the whole thing. Gram never said a word, but the telltale stains seeped through the mortise joints.

"You don't need to be spending all your time helping Gram, Billy James. That stubborn woman coulda moved in here with us years ago, instead of stayin' in that no-better-than-a-chicken-shack cabin of hers."

This was an ancient fester with Mama. One I wasn't gonna argue over, though I thought it pretty short-sighted of her not to understand. "Yep," I said, stuffing the last achy-sweet bite into my mouth.

It wasn't the cabin, anyhow. It was the land that kept Gram there. The land and what had gone before.

Palm Springs had left by the time I arrived. Gram sent me up the ladder without one word about her midnight boarder. I frowned around the nails caught in my teeth and kept working.

By noon my bare back dripped sweat and my hair steamed against my scalp. I took a sip from my water bottle and surveyed the job. I'd stripped Ray's patches first thing. No hard feat. He had used plain old nails, not galvanized, and they'd rusted right out of the roof. I had scraped off the warped shingles and tacked down new, making sure to overlap them just so.

"*Caw!*"

At the far corner of the roof, a raven danced along the flashing, appraised me with coal-black eyes, then flicked its tail and flapped straight up into the blue sky. I stood and wiped my brow.

*THUMP!*

"Agggh!" I spasmed and pitched forward.

With teeth clenched, I rubbed my throbbing shoulder blade. The rock that struck my back clattered onto the roof and rolled into the gutter.

Laughter.

"You best be done, Gnat!"

Ray.

Holding my breath, I stood just enough to peek into the yard.

Amend that. Ray and Company J.

J for jerks—Tray and Beavis.

I squatted and chewed my scab. Ray wouldn't do much with Gram looking on. If there's one thing he could be counted on for, it was his predictability. I'd known he'd come looking for me today. I'd mouthed off plenty yesterday. Better to face him at Gram's.

After pulling my shirt on, I duckwalked to the ladder, shoulders tense, waiting for another missile as I climbed down.

"'Bout time. Didn't take *me* four hours to patch that chicken coop."

I jumped the last three rungs. "What do you want, Ray?"

He was on me in a flash, fist twisted in my shirt. My feet lifted off the ground as Ray pulled me into his apple-red pimply face.

"I want some respect from you, Gnat. That's what I want. Thought you might've figured that out yesterday, but I guess you need another lesson."

"Raymond Clay."

He dropped me like a sack of feed. His lip curled into a plastic smile as he turned to face Gram. "Good ole Gram. Ever watchful on her mountaintop."

Snickers.

"Dontcha mean hilltop, Ray?" said Beavis.

'Course his real name wasn't Beavis, it was Parker. Parker Waldorf. But no one in Kelseyville would be caught dead with a name like Parker Waldorf, so Ray called him Beavis. Logically, everyone else did, too.

Ray laughed and brushed a hank of red hair out of his face. "That's right. Hilltop." He kicked up a cloud of dust and pebbles. "Rocky hilltop. Sounds like a song, don't it?"

They all laughed.

"Billy James," Gram said, waving specks of dust out of her eyes, "you've done enough work here for one day. Get on down the hill before your mama gets home."

Ray clapped a hand to my burning back. "We'll drive you, Gnat. No need to strain your precious footsies."

"No, sir, Raymond Clay."

We all turned to Gram, who had her hands on wide hips, square jaw set. Chickens pecked at scraps she'd dumped over the side of the porch rail. "I need some strong, fresh lads to set by some kindlin'."

Ray snorted and eyed Gram warily, but no one left. Those hard eyes pinned them where they stood. "Get on! Axe's over by the coop." Her gaze crashed onto Ray, and I watched with glee as Ray squirmed. "The *chicken* coop."

"But, Gram! I've got important things—"

"You refusing me help, boy?"

Ray stiffened. "No, ma'am."

"Hmph. I thought not." Gram walked into the house, and I lit out, leaving my tools behind without a second thought.

# CHAPTER 4

ike the water tower, the loft in our barn was a passable private space. Ray would be gunning for me
all over again after today's episode at Gram's, but
the loft was as good a place as any to avoid him. I had
comics stashed in there, too, along with other things: an
ancient blue pop bottle, chunks of quartz from
Culloden Crick, an arrowhead, and twelve silver dollars
from Gram—one for each birthday.

Then there was Gloria's box, which I'd stashed in
the loft after dropping off Palm Springs last night. Time
to find the glue and make those repairs.

Ducking to keep from hitting my head against the
pulley beam, I shinnied down the ladder to the barn
floor. Cammy, our milk cow, gazed at me with tired
brown eyes, then looked away. People did that a lot—
looked away when I came into a room, as if looking at
me might taint them with the same stain that had dirt-
ied Gloria.

After patting Cammy's damp nose, I shooed Mama's
Rhode Island Reds outside and jogged through to the
adjacent workroom. Each tool, can of spray paint, rag,

and nut or bolt had its proper place. I had about four projects going right now. A cuckoo clock for Mrs. Westerfield. A CD player for Hog. And two messed-up toasters. Those were both for Mrs. Fitzsimmons. She went through toasters quicker than we went through gallons of milk. I still wasn't sure what she kept trying to jam into them—sandwiches, maybe.

Guess you were allowed to do things like that when you were ninety-two and pretty much blind. I just kept fixing them up, giving them back, and taking the next broken one to repair.

I reached for the glue, which should have been on the third shelf right of the door, but it wasn't. In fact, after five minutes of searching, it became obvious the glue wasn't in the shed at all.

Mama must've taken it. Probably needed to glue a dish and forgot to put it back.

With one eye on the road (no way I wanted Ray sneaking up on me), I ran for the house. The kitchen was my first stop. I shuffled cleaners aside and reached into the dark recesses of the under-sink hole, but no glue. Where would she have put it? Her room, maybe?

I dashed upstairs and scanned the bookshelves lining her wall. You'd think there'd be books on bookshelves, but not in Mama's room. Her shelves were covered with plates. That's right, plates. Commemorative plates of all kinds of places and things. There was one from Niagara Falls, one from Washington, D.C., one from some place in Kansas called The Big Well. All places Mama'd never set foot in or on.

She was a member of an exchange club that sent

each other plates from places all over the country. Like in Terrington, Nevada's historic Train Depot 99, or Little Penny's Candy Emporium. I learned more about obscure American historical sites and buildings from reading Mama's plates than I ever did from a book.

I moved a plate or two, looking for a chip of plaster or bone china, anything that would indicate a need for repair. Nothing. Then I turned and saw it, half buried behind a stack of letters and bills on her dresser. Its orange cap stuck out like a road cone.

Envelopes tumbled to the floor as I plucked it from the pile. Bills: water, power, gas. They had little dates scribbled in their left-hand corners. June 6th, May 30th.

My gaze strayed to a familiar name—mine.

*Return to Sender* was marked in black ink across the front.

I stared at the hand-printed return address and frowned. I didn't know any M. Porter. Or anyone in . . . Blaeloch, Tennessee? The seal was unopened, but the edges were slightly ripped, and there was a smudge of—

My hand found the glue in my pocket.

Had Mama opened my letter, then reglued it?

It was addressed to me, even if I didn't know who it was from. It had my name on it. *Why would she do something like that?*

SLAM!

"Billy James!"

*MAMA.*

I shoved the envelope into the pile and skittered out the door and down the hall, stopping at the top of the stairs just as her tired face peered up.

"Raymond Clay said you lit out on Gram when it

came time to do her chopping. That true?"

*Tattletale.* It was hard to believe Ray was eighteen and not eight. "No, ma'am. Well, I did leave when Gram asked Ray to split, but that's because I'd already spent—"

Her eyes narrowed and I swallowed the guilty rush of words. Not guilt over Gram; guilt at snooping in Mama's room.

"Billy James, you know your brother's too old to be waiting on Gram hand and foot. He's things to do, working and all like he does. I've told your Gram, but she turns a deaf ear, so I expect you to do what's right, hear? What were you thinking, running off like that?"

My spine stiffened, but I kept my mouth shut. Ray'd gotten to her first.

She shook her head and rubbed her back. "I am too tired, Billy James, to deal with this nonsense from you boys."

As Mama turned and started toward the kitchen, I leaned against the railing and let out a shaky breath.

*Damn Ray. Damn him to hell and further still, as Gloria used to say.*

# CHAPTER 5

unday was church day. Well, and baseball, but that came after church. We were there early because Mama served the Bible Study group coffee and biscuits, and I passed out bulletins at the door. After the ten a.m. service, we went to Sunday school, then Mama helped prepare the eleven-thirty luncheon. By the time we got home from eating and cleaning up, it was past two, over half the day given up to a God that paid no mind to any of us Wilkinses.

"Billy James!"

Sue Anne Stoddard skipped over, her orange hair glistening in the early morning sun like prairie grass at sunset. "You look so handsome in that suit and tie, Billy." Her teeth shone pearly white. I scratched the back of my neck, pulling at the damp collar.

"Uh, thanks. And you look"—I grimaced—"nice, too."

Her smile widened, blue eyes sparkling like I'd said she was Queen of the May. "Why, thank you." She twirled, the pink pleated skirt flaring above her knees. "Mama said this skirt was perfect to accentuate my slender figure."

My face burned red as Sue Anne's hair. The girl

acted like she was Raymond Clay's age, talking about her figure this, her complexion that. Mama didn't have a high opinion of Sue Anne *or* her mama for letting her wallow in appearances.

"Why, Billy James, is that a blush I see?"

*Slap!* A hand hit my shoulder. Thankfully, the one without the bruise.

I turned to glare into the grinning face of—Hog! My savior, the only friend who hadn't abandoned me after Gloria's explosion of weirdness. We knocked knuckles, then hooked fingers.

"How's it hangin', Gnat?"

It was okay when Hog called me Gnat. I was Gnat and he was Hog. Both names christened by Ray. "S'goin', Hog."

I heard a "hmph" from behind and hazarded a glance at Sue Anne. Her lip curled like an angry dog's. "You two are intolerable together!" She turned and flounced away, much to my relief.

Hog grinned and hooked a finger in his nose, pretending to flick one at Sue Anne's retreating back.

"Man, you got here just in time."

"Don't I know it." Hog pulled me into the alcove and shoved a wad of bulletins in my hands. "Compliments of my dad."

Preacher Cal Sterkam was Hog's daddy, all two hundred and ninety pounds of him. When Preacher Cal said, "Hand out these bulletins with a smile!" you smiled till your face cracked. If he said, "Get down on your knees and beg for salvation!" you fell right to your knees and praised the Almighty.

God was a big deal in Kelseyville, and the people demanded a strong voice in the pulpit. According to Mama, Preacher Cal was a mouthpiece for God. I guess he did an okay job of it, since he'd been the preacher for near twenty years, and his grandfather was our preacher before that. It must've been in their blood.

I snuck a glance at Hog, all squirmy and twitchy by the door. Well, maybe it skipped generations. He was thrusting out bulletins rapid-fire, knowin' the quicker he pawned them off, the sooner we could quit inspection.

People poured in and I went into robot mode, handing out bulletins with a grin and a greeting, "Nice to see you Mr. and Mrs. So and So."

Before Gloria died, I generally heard back, "Lands! But you've grown 'bout a mile, Billy James. Your mama must be so proud!"

But since Gloria's passing, it was more like: "Well, it's nice to see you here, Billy James." Or, "You're a good, God-fearin' boy. . . ." As if I needed extra support to keep from traveling down the same dark road as Gloria.

The choir belted out "By the Hand of Jesus" while the last of the latecomers found their seats. The door opened and two more stragglers shuffled in. Hog thrust out a bulletin along with his plastic smile, but my heart stopped beating; my breath refused to come.

It was Palm Springs. All dressed up in a suit and tie, looking like it was choking him where he stood. His eyes spit fire, his lips clamped so tight I wondered if they might split his face in two.

"Thank you, Mr. Sterkam," the lady said to Hog. The boy didn't notice me as the woman steered his stiff body through the sanctuary doors and over to a pew at the back of the church.

After the ushers closed the inner doors, Hog leaned in, eyebrows raised. "Wow. First time I've seen her out anywhere since . . . well, you know. And who's that pudgy kid with her?"

"Beats me," I squeaked, wondering how the heck Gram's boarder ended up at church with Gloria Russell's mama.

I cornered the boy in the bathroom after Sunday school. Actually, I'd followed him as soon as he made a run for it. He was stripping off his tie when I eased inside. His eyes widened in recognition, then narrowed like a rabid wolf right before it set to ripping out your throat.

"It's all your fault!" he yelled, his lower lip thrust out. "She watches me every second now."

"What are you doin' here with Ms. Russell?"

He snorted, shoved his tie into the trashcan, then rubbed a hand over his neatly combed hair. "You stupid, or what?"

My face burned. Hillbilly was one thing; stupid was another. "Look, all I want to know is why you're here with Ms. Russell."

His left eye twitched, and he licked his lips. "You should know."

"All I know is you're a city boy with no sense of direction." I couldn't resist the dig, but felt bad as soon as his eyes hit the floor.

But they came back up poppin' with anger. "Fine. You can keep on wondering!"

He yanked the door open and fled. A cry of "Hillbilly!" hit my ears in his wake.

I had to find out the truth, even if it meant asking Sue Anne.

I prayed it wouldn't come to that.

I should have known there was no chance a Wilkins's prayer would be answered. Sue Anne was sitting next to me, a satisfied smile on her lips. I had chosen a table as close to Ms. Russell and the boy (whose name I still didn't know) as possible, hoping to "eavesdrop" my way to an answer.

Palm Springs kicked his feet against the legs of the metal chair, lip thrust out, a full plate of untouched food in front of him. Ms. Russell picked at her food, her face pale. The boy sneaked longing glances at the juicy pieces of fried chicken and potato salad, gnawing his lip harder by the second. If he didn't break down soon, I figured he might swallow himself whole.

Would serve the brat right.

Sue Anne dabbed at her mouth with a napkin and politely asked me to pass the salt. Don't know why I kept looking for Hog. He'd left already for baseball practice. No one to save my soul this time.

My thoughts tripped back to Preacher Cal's sermon about not being seduced by soothsayers and traffickers of the supernatural to solve our problems. Preacher Cal was always big on lecturing about resisting "temptation" and the "devil," but even so, the sermon left a weird knot in my chest.

"Can you believe Gloria's mama had the nerve to

come?" whispered a minty-scented mouth next to my ear.

I tried not to yank my head into reverse. "Uh, well, I figure it's about time she started getting back to things. Don't you?"

Sue Anne's lips pursed. "Well, I guess she'd have to at *some* point. But my mama said if it were her, she'd have packed up and moved on. No use staying somewhere full of bad memories and—" She stopped and looked at her mama, who was deep in conversation with Patsy Simpson, chicken skin hanging from their fingers. Their gazes flicked in Ms. Russell's direction every so often.

"And what?" I asked.

She leaned in. "And dangerous atmospheres." Her eyes strayed to Ms. Russell and the boy. "And to think she brought him here to stay with her! Now of all times. Well, my mama says that's just plain crazy."

"Sue Anne!" came a fierce whisper. Mrs. Stoddard raised her feathery eyebrows. "Are you gossipin', Suzybee? Now, you know how I feel about that."

Sue Anne sighed and rolled her eyes. "Yes, Mama."

I had a few bites of potato salad while Sue Anne pretended to sip her iced tea. Mrs. Stoddard got up to refill her plate, and Sue Anne leaned back in. "As I was sayin', Ms. Russell must be out of her mind, bringing him here, of all places. It's like she has a death wish for *all* her children."

I froze. Had I heard her right? I took a moment to study his face, his eyes, the shape of his mouth. No. *How is that possible?*

"You didn't know?" she said.

"What? Oh, sure. She, ah, mentioned him plenty of times. Said what a brat he was." I felt like giggling, for some crazy, out-of-control reason. Like God played another big joke on me. Another way of saying, "How many times you gonna be a fool, Billy James?"

Sue Anne smiled, those perfect teeth shining. "We'll see how long he lasts here. He's a city boy, you know, living with his Daddy like he has. I bet he and his mama both end up leaving Kelseyville. Which would be best, don't you think?"

All I could do was nod and stare at the kid that apparently everyone knew about but me. Me, who should have known that my best friend for over six years had a brother living in California.

# CHAPTER 6

brother. An *eight*-year-old little brother. Which meant he'd been about two when Gloria and her mama moved to Kelseyville. What type of mama leaves her tot behind, then sets out for another state? Dads do that kind of thing, but moms? It seemed unbelievable. Weird, like maybe it couldn't be true.

I scuffed my feet through the limestone gravel on the road, sending up chalky plumes of dust. Why hadn't Gloria ever mentioned him? And why hadn't he come for the funeral?

It was no big surprise when Gloria's daddy didn't show. Gloria had told me her daddy had no use for her and her mama. In fact, he'd kicked them out when she'd been only six. Gloria's mama had gone back to her old last name, and changed Gloria's right along with it.

They'd ended up in Kelseyville because that was where her mama had been raised. People always seem to go back to what they know in times of trouble.

The rusted brown of the water tower loomed above the tree line to my left, but suddenly I didn't want to climb that rickety ladder or sit on that familiar splintered deck. I forced my legs to walk back the direction I'd just come.

"Why didn't you tell me, Gloria?" I whispered, thinking about the box I'd re-glued yesterday. I hadn't seen what was inside since the last time Gloria read the new poem she'd written.

She made me swear not to open it unless "something untoward happens to me." I had to look up that word, "untoward." It meant something unpleasant. Something like dying would qualify as "untoward," I guessed. And yet three weeks later, I still hadn't opened it. Maybe there was more in there than poems, half-melted antique bottles, and bits of Indian pottery. Maybe there was stuff in there about her brother. And her dad. And maybe even about Satan.

I swallowed thickly as my eyes shifted across the open field to the rocky, tree-lined hills beyond. They jutted up from the valley like hairy, knotted knuckles. Satan lived on his own knob, opposite Gram's, 'bout half an hour walk between them.

Had they ever made that walk to call on one another? Doubtful. And if I was to ask Gram, I'd only get that black and narrow "What business is it of yours?" look.

None. None of my business. Just like Gloria's box. And Gloria's brother.

But there *was* something that was my business. That letter that Mama was keeping from me was my business. And it would have to be sent back tomorrow. Monday. Question was, how could I get it out of the mailbox before Mr. Cathcart picked up the mail?

I made a run for the water tower. The ladder creaked and twisted under my clumsy scramble to the top. But as soon as I sat on the deck and looked out through the crooked branches of the oak to the countryside below, my head calmed right down. The old tree's twisted arms were getting ready to puncture the rusted tin straight through. Wherever there were old buildings, gnarly trees grew against them, not so much intruding as holding things up.

Gripping the splintery edge, I let out a heavy breath.

Now I could think. Plan. I was gonna find out who Mr. M. Porter from Tennessee was, why he was writing to me, and why Mama didn't think I needed to know.

Took me a while, but I figured the plan out. Gloria was the plotting mastermind, but I had picked up a thing or two in six years.

Mrs. Petranski's tan, thin face loomed over me. "You do look pale, Billy. No fever, though. It's your stomach, you say?"

"Yes, ma'am. It's all queasy and, uh, crampy." I twitched like a spasm was wrapping me into a pretzel right there on the school nurse's olive-green cot.

"Well, I can see you're not in good shape at all. Let's call your mama at home and see what she wants you to do."

That was the easy part. Getting Mama to say "Go on and send him home" would be harder. I hoped Mrs. Petranski had it in her to insist.

"Mrs. Wilkins? Yes, this is Nurse Petranski from school. Billy's here and he's complaining of a powerful stomach-ache." She tapped her painted nails on the desk. "What? No, no fever, but . . . yes, right, but he's—"

I moaned and curled my knees to my chest. Her eyes widened. "But Mrs. Wilkins, I really think he needs to be at home. There are several cases of the stomach flu going around, and he won't be able to do much work in the condition he's in now."

A long pause. "Yes, just a minute." She smiled thinly and handed me the phone. "She'd like to speak with you."

Oh, no. I cradled the phone between ear and shoulder, trying to maintain my pain-filled voice without overdoing it. "Mama?"

"Billy James. What's going on? You were fine when you left this morning."

Fatal flaw. Gloria would have picked up on it right away. She would have said, "Now don't forget to do some casual complainin' when you go down for breakfast. Gotta set things up."

Dang it. "I did feel okay earlier, Mama." Couldn't lie about that now. "But an hour ago my stomach started crampin' something awful. I tried to stick it out, but, I, well, I thought I might embarrass myself if I stayed in the classroom, you know?"

"Lord Almighty, Billy James, if every kid came home when he had to pass gas, the school would be empty five days a week."

"That's the problem." I looked at Mrs. Petranski and lowered my voice. "I haven't been able to pass any. It's all blocked up in there, Mama. Maybe if I come home, I can work some of it out, then come back?"

Silence for a moment. "Billy James, you are gonna be the death of me. All right, hand me back to that nurse."

I did, feeling dizzy with triumph. I heard: "Hold on a second. Will you be able to walk home, Billy? Or does your mom need to come pick you up?"

"I'll walk."

# CHAPTER 7

**Y**ou could set your clock by Mama's schedule. She finished her shower by six, cooked breakfast, then put the mail out at nine, even though Mr. Cathcart showed up near noon. I didn't dare fish around in the box on my way *to* the house. Mama would be watching for me. That meant I had an hour to fake "getting it all out of my system" before heading back to school and making a quick stop at the mailbox first.

If I was lucky, she'd be deep into cleaning by the time I left. Nothing could pull Mama away from her morning chores once she got started.

I trudged up the road, trying hard not to look like a kid faking ill just to go home early and carry on mischief. Hog had given me the "What's up?" head flick when I'd left class. A part of me wanted to tell him about the letter, about my plans, but I couldn't bring myself to do it.

So intent was I on my thoughts, I didn't see him till the rhythmic flapping of his coat brought my head up. My head felt heavy with the sudden rush of blood.

*Mr. Satan.* On the road. Four yards ahead, moving

right for me. I scrambled to the opposite side of the narrow lane. My dash caused him to look up, his eyes widening in surprise.

I had never been close enough to see his eyes. They were blue, like the sky in mid-April, or the bubblegum ice cream at Swenson's in Windell. His gaze shot down to the ground, and he hunched over, as if trying to make himself smaller.

My feet crunched to a halt.

He stopped, too, his coat coming to rest against the back of his calves like a tangled flag. He lifted his head and all I could do was stare at his eyes. His gaze felt as if it were a breezy touch on my forehead, running down past my cracked lip to my square chin. Something stirred in my chest, and the hairs on the back of my neck sizzled, sending crazy pings down my spine.

I couldn't breathe, couldn't speak, couldn't move. My feet had grown roots, anchoring me to that strip of roadway.

He smiled a sad, crooked smile, then passed on by.

My insides twisted about themselves as if I'd eaten twenty-five cinnamon gobstoppers in under an hour. When my legs finally unfroze, I turned and Satan was gone. My gaze zoomed over the roadway and nearby countryside.

*Where was he?*

The drainage ditch was on one side, a straggly stand of birch and scrub oak on the other, but I saw no coat, no tall, bobbing head.

What if he were laying up for me? Doubling back to head me off before I got home? I envisioned his lanky arms squeezing me in a death hug, and my legs grew wings. I flew the entire five blocks, my aches and pain, real and fake, forgotten.

No need to convince Mama I was in dire straits for real. From my permanent position on the toilet, it was obvious there was more stewing inside me than half-truths.

I wiped sweat from my face for the hundredth time and blew out a stale puff of air.

"Come on out, Billy James. Isn't anything left that you can afford to give up at this point."

That was true. I washed my hands and eased into the hallway where Mama was waiting for me.

"Here." She handed me a small bowl of soda crackers. "Go lie down. You won't be goin' back to school today."

I sat. "Mama? I—I think I can eat this, then head on back."

Her head popped in, the lines around her mouth deep as canyons. "Are you playing games with me, Billy James?"

My heart skipped a beat. "No, ma'am. I just don't want a lot of makeup work."

The lines softened to low valleys. "Plenty of time to catch up on missed work after school tomorrow. You rest now."

She walked out, closing the door behind her. I stared at the bowl for a full three minutes before I thought to set it on the nightstand. No way I could eat.

The blue numbers on my clock read 11:32. I had to figure something out quick. The mailbox gleamed in the late morning sun outside the window, and my eyes searched the roadway for any sign of Mr. Cathcart's Jeep. I hadn't planned on *really* being stuck on the toilet for over an hour, and since I wasn't going back to school, there was no way I could stroll out the front door and shove my hand into the mailbox.

My fingers drummed on the windowsill as I willed my mind to come up with something brilliant. What would Gloria do?

The clank and swish of hot water rushing through our pipes told me that Mama had resumed cleaning. I flicked the latch and opened the window, a warm breeze tickling my nose. Climbing down wouldn't be a problem, but getting back up would be harder. And I would have to be quiet like a mouse.

If she caught me . . .

I shuddered at the thought, then straightened when I imagined Gloria's frown. *Take control of your life, Billy!* That had been one of the last things she had said to me, but seeing what "taking control" of *her* life had led to, I wasn't of a mind to listen at the time. But now—

Without giving my brain time to reconsider, I pulled the screen inside, stashed it under the bed, then eased myself onto the porch roof. The shingles were dry and splintery under my fingers and feet, but solid. I inched my way to the edge of the awning.

The water stopped running, and I froze. Pots banged and clashed their way into the sink, and the scrubbing started up again. I breathed a sigh of relief and peeked into the yard.

Not a soul in sight, and no Jeep—yet. I crept over to

one of the main porch columns. The plaster was cool against my bare feet. Wrapping both arms around the pillar, I shinnied down at breakneck speed.

My feet hit the compact dirt with a muffled thump. I ducked, my heart trying to break free of my rib cage.

*Only ten yards to the mailbox, Billy, ten yards.*

I listened for the reassuring clang of dishes, but it was eerily silent. Had she gone upstairs? The thought started the cramps all over again.

Then I saw it: a telltale plume of yellow dust rolling in from the west like a fast-approaching summer storm. Without another thought, I popped up and ran, my legs moving in what felt like slow motion as I kept one eye on the dust cloud, the other on the mailbox. Too bad there weren't eyes in the back of my head to see if Mama had come to the front window and spotted my twisted sprint across the lawn.

Actually, better not to see that. Who in their right mind would want to look certain death in the face? Other than Gloria, that is.

With one final lunge, my hand fastened on the latch and I yanked it down. The box was full. Bills. A letter to Aunt Gessie.

My eyes rose. The dust cloud was only yards away.

*Where was it?*

My fingers shook as I shuffled frantically through the pile. *Don't tell me she didn't put it*—there it was—my name written in bold black letters. I shoved it into my pocket.

The battered Jeep, red with faded chrome, was coming into sight. I flew across the yard to the side of the house, ducking behind Mama's peony bushes. Mr. Cathcart's brakes screeched as he came to a lurching halt. He looked around briefly, then opened the box and went about his normal routine.

*He hadn't seen me.*

The front screen banged. Heavy footsteps fell on the porch before I spotted Mama walking toward the mailbox.

No way I'd make it to my window with her outside. And if I waited till she went in, there was the chance she'd get to my room before I could find a way back up.

Only one other choice.

Sprinting to the back door, I slipped inside, scrambled through the kitchen, and ran for the stairs. Almost to the top.

"Billy James? What are you doin' out of bed?"

*Lie to her, Billy,* echoed Gloria's voice as if she were standing right next to me.

My hands twisted together as I turned. "I wanted more crackers but forgot my bowl."

She frowned. "Don't be eatin' too much too quickly. We want it to stay in, not come right back out."

I nodded. Good thing she couldn't see my face as I walked up the rest of the way. Good thing all the way around that I was still breathing.

The bed creaked beneath my butt as I sat and exhaled. *Not bad.* I could feel Gloria's satisfied smile. The letter crinkled in my pocket and I pulled it out, my fingers shaking. When the water started up again, I ran a finger behind the crusty seal. The note inside was written on plain old notebook paper, the handwriting tight and businesslike.

*Dear Billy,*

*I've gotten back two other letters, so I can only hope you get the opportunity to read this one before your mama sends it back. I won't say one bad word about your mama. She's done wonders with you boys all on her own this whole time.*

*I've kept my distance, respecting your mama's wishes to raise you boys without interference, but time's passed, and I think you need to know you have a grandfather who cares about you.*

Grandfather?

I knew I had one out there somewhere, but since Daddy left when I was only a baby, I never gave much thought to whether or not his daddy would have a lick of interest in me or Raymond Clay. Why should he if his son didn't?

I forced my eyes back to the letter:

*I was hoping your mama would see it the same way, but looks like she's not going to bend.*

*That being the case, I'll keep writing, hoping you might pick up the mail one day and have an opportunity to read what I have to say. I'll be the first to say your mama didn't deserve the type of treatment she got from my boy. He always was a wild one, never listening to anything or anyone. Not that I'm making excuses, but looking back now, I think your daddy never felt up to the same level as other folks. Truth is, I feel responsible for that, but by the time he was a man, wasn't a thing I could say that would put him in the mind to listen.*

*It might have been more of a blessing that he left. That might be hard for you to hear, Billy, but it's God's own truth. I don't know how much your mama has told you about your daddy, but he had some real problems. Problems with the bottle to bury his feelings, problems controlling his temper. Your daddy chose a hard road.*

It sounded like he was describing Ray. *My* Raymond Clay, not *his* Raymond Clay. The thought made me cold all over, and sort of excited. Mama didn't talk about Daddy. Ray never talked about him either, even though he was about six when Daddy left and he must have remembered *something*.

*I want you to know, Billy, I'll be here if you need me. I haven't had any better luck contacting your brother. He seems to have no interest in hearing what I have to say.*

*My home is open to you. Perhaps one summer I can convince your mama to let you come and stay a spell. We could visit your daddy's grave and let you pay your respects. Sometimes that's important for a boy, to have some finality.*

*Well, I guess that's about all.*

*Sarah, if you read this, please find it in your heart to share it with Billy. The boy deserves to know he has relatives outside of Kelseyville.*

*Love,*
*Micah Porter*

I let the letter fall into my lap, hardly able to take it all in. I knew my daddy had died. Mama told me that years ago. Best I could piece together was that he had taken off when I was a baby, then got himself killed about a year later. I didn't know how he died, or where he was buried.

My head sunk into the pillow as I collapsed back onto the bed. So my daddy's last name had been Porter. Mama had gone back to her maiden name after Daddy left, changing our names right along with hers.

"Billy James Porter." It sounded wrong coming off my lips, like a betrayal. I shoved the letter back into the envelope and hid it under the mattress.

# CHAPTER 8

riday nights at Greystokes weren't the same without Gloria.

My thoughts eased back to last spring. Our regular routine consisted of filching pomegranates from Mr. Finnegan's tree that overhung the diner's rickety back fence, then seeing who could spit the pits closest to his lazy black hound's rear end without rousing him from his coma. Or even just sitting on the steps and listening to Cat play until the wee hours.

I sat out front until the sun tiptoed behind the hills, then went inside. Most Greystokes regulars were still sweet as Gram's butterscotch pudding to me: "Now, aren't you a good boy to be helpin' out your mama, Billy James?" Or, "Time heals all wounds, Billy James." Or for some people, "You stop by sometime this week, Billy. I've got a squeaky door I'd like you to take a look at." But since Gloria died, there was something in their words. Something I couldn't quite put my finger on, but standing still and giving them their say made my toes curl.

Which was what I had to do about ten times before I could work my way over to Cat. Last to glom on to me was Preacher Cal. He and Mrs. Sterkam claimed the center table. The other tables and booths seemed to cluster 'round his like cattle crowding a watering hole. 'Course Hog wasn't with them. Friday nights he went to Windell to spend time with his mama and stepdaddy.

Preacher Cal thrust out a hand to stop my progress. "Whoa there, tiger. Where's the fire?"

His toothy grin had the same effect. My toes curled right there in my worn-out Keds. His gaze dropped to the floor, and I thought he might've been able to see them, all bunched up against the blue canvas. But no, he was looking at something on the high-polished linoleum.

He bent down, then held something next to my cheek. Three or four one dollar bills.

"I think these must be yours, Billy James," Preacher Cal said. He tucked the bills into my shirt pocket, his clean-shaven face split in a wide grin. My eyes cut to Mrs. Sterkam. She was staring all googly at Preacher Cal, as if he'd just saved some poor drowning kitten.

*Say something, Billy.*

"Uh . . . thanks."

Preacher Cal waved a hand. "It's nothing. Every young man should have a little spending money, right?" He paused and looked around. His audience beamed back and nodded. Preacher Cal leaned in, his voice low. "It's always good to know who your friends are, Billy James." He patted my head, scrunching my hair down over my eyes. "Run along now."

Dismissed like a faithful hound.

I managed to lurch to the stage, where Cat sat tuning his guitar. His rusty brown hair hid part of his face.

Had he seen me take the money? It wasn't like I wanted it. Or was even given a choice.

His head rose at my approach. We slapped hands, then hooked fingers. I sat on the plywood steps that served as a stage and watched the regulars trickle in while he tuned. You could tell from their faces that they were looking forward to their usual dose of home-brewed Greystokes malt, Jammin' Cat's soulful serenade, and a slice of Mama's boysenberry pie.

"How's it goin', little man?" Cat asked as he plucked at strings and twisted knobs.

"Okay, I guess."

He looked at me sideways. "You guess? You don't sound too sure."

I shrugged.

He pulled at the maroon tie around his neck, loosening it. "You feelin' down about Gloria?"

Cat was sharp. "Not really about Gloria, but it's related to her. Did you know Gloria had a little brother, Cat?"

His long fingers froze above the strings. "How'd you find out 'bout that?"

My mouth dried up. "You—*you knew*?"

He clucked his tongue and laid the guitar flat across his knees. His pale eyes scanned the room. I figured he was making sure no one was close enough to get an earful before he leaned in. "Well, it's like this, Billy, and you're not to repeat what I say, understand?"

I nodded, my fingers clenched tight enough to draw blood.

Lowering his voice, he said, "I knew only 'cause Ms. Russell came in here one night 'bout a year ago and imbibed a smidgen too much. I was playin' my heavy blues back then, the kind that make ya wanna spill your soul, ya know?"

I knew.

"Well, she up and started wailing 'bout her 'boy,' and what a terrible mother she was to allow her ex to keep him from her this whole time. 'A boy needs his mama, don't you think, Cat?' she kept sayin'."

Cat leaned back and wiped a hand over his lean face. "She talked a lot that night, Billy, and all I could do was listen, then put her in the sheriff's car to be taken home. Never mentioned anything she said, 'cause I didn't think it was none of my business. Figured if Gloria had wanted us to know about her little brother, she woulda said somethin'." He eyed me. "So, how'd you find out?"

"Everyone knows. Not just me."

An eyebrow shot up. "That so?"

"Yes." I explained about Palm Springs and his appearance at church. Cat took it all in without interrupting once. "What I can't figure is why she never told me. Why would she hide that?"

He looked thoughtful, rubbing thumb and forefinger over his clean-shaven chin. It was usually pretty stubbly on a Friday, and I figured his sweetheart being in town had something to do with his put-together appearance. "I don't rightly have an answer to that, little man. I imagine she had her reasons, though." His eyes bored into me. "Fact is, we all have a secret or two we don't want shared. It's just the way of people, to keep what's most likely to hurt them close to their chest."

"You sound like Gloria!" I said in exasperation.

Cat chuckled and propped his guitar back on his knee. "Well, now, why d'you think we got on so well?"

"It's just that none of it makes any sense. Gloria dyin' like she did, and her keepin' that secret about her little brother. And people thinkin' that—that Sata—"

His callused hand rested on my arm. "Billy, knowing the full truth don't always make sense, but it *can* change you. Truth always changes a body. It's just the nature of the beast."

My heart knocked into my throat as I thought of the letter, and Gloria's box.

Cat dropped his hand and leaned forward. "Listen, Billy, a twelve-year-old girl dyin' from an aneurysm may not be the easiest explanation for folks to digest, but those doctors knew what they was talkin' about. There's no great mystery here, 'cept . . ." Cat's amber eyes raised slightly, and a wicked shiver passed down my spine.

He looked back at his guitar and strummed a mellow chord. "Well, let's just leave it be." He smiled, his grin reaching all the way to his eyes. "Time for me to earn my pay, little man. I got a woman who wants to go out tomorrow night." He winked, and I grinned back. I liked Darla, Cat's girlfriend. She lived in Branson but was fixing to move to Kelseyville once she and Cat tied the knot. Not only was she pretty, she laughed easy and loud. Which is why I figured Cat liked her so much.

I leaned back on my elbows and waited to get lost in Cat's mellow tunes. His fingers strummed a few chords, then picked out an uncomplicated rhythm. The hum and buzz of the diner flowed around Cat's playin', like a tractor plowing next to a brook.

Soon his husky voice hovered over the crowd like rain clouds after a wearisome dry spell. Some people had stopped chatting, their attention fixed—if not directly on Cat, then on the space around him.

I realized they were seeing the shape of the tune, feeling the truth of his words. Surprise filled me. Gloria had said most didn't "get it" about Cat's music and I had been inclined to agree, since Cat wasn't paid much, nor did people praise him like he deserved. But as heads bopped, eyes closed, and fingers and feet tapped, it occurred to me that maybe Gloria had been wrong. Some townsfolk *did* get it.

I looked at Preacher Cal's table. Mr. Williams, his wife, and Mr. Finnegan had joined the preacher and Mrs. Sterkam. Hog's stepmama and Mrs. Williams were tapping their feet, eyes all dreamy. Mr. Williams, Mr. Finnegan, and Preacher Cal were deep in conversation. I could tell it was serious by the hunched set to their shoulders.

Preacher Cal leaned back, a sober look on his usually jovial face. "Don't be so stubborn now, Dennis. This is a golden opportunity."

Mr. Williams banged a fist on the table. "You think I could stomach even a minute with him?"

"Calm down, Dennis." Mr. Finnegan put a hand on Mr. Williams's shoulder. "You gotta look at the bigger—"

Mr. Williams was out of his chair so fast, it nearly toppled to the floor. The hairs on the back of my neck stood on end. He yanked his wallet out of his back pocket, threw a bill onto the table, then pulled out his wife's chair. "Let's go, Candy."

She got up, a confused look on her face. "Dennis? What's—"

His hand fastened on her wrist, and their eyes locked. "Now, please." It was almost a whisper, but I knew what he'd said. Read it right off his lips. His wife reached down and grabbed her purse. She whispered something to Mrs. Sterkam on her way down. Sorry, maybe?

Preacher Cal stood. "Dennis. Please, don't go."

Mr. Williams waved a hand and avoided the preacher's steady gaze. "Not now, Cal. I gotta get out of here."

And they did. Walked right through the crowd (who were all watchin', not even trying to pretend they weren't, like me) and out the front door.

Cat didn't miss a beat. Kept right on strummin' as if nothing had happened. Which, by the way everyone went back to their meals and conversations, I guess nothing had.

# CHAPTER 9

After Cat's second set, I went into the kitchen to get him a glass of tea and something to eat.

My mind was still stumbling over the scene at Preacher Cal's table as I parted the swinging doors and entered the clash and bang of the brightly lit kitchen. I stopped, my Keds squeaking on the waxed linoleum.

Sue Anne was standing at the pastry block kneading biscuits next to Mama. *What in the holy heck is she doing?* Sue Anne came to Greystokes on occasion, but she didn't make it a practice to hang out in the kitchen.

Spotting me, she yanked her hands out of the doughy lump lightning fast. "Oh! Billy's here." She flicked her wrists, sending plumes of flour dust into the air. "Thanks for the lesson, Ms. Wilkins," she said, all respectful-like as she wiped her hands on a towel Mama handed her.

Mama looked ready to spit, but all she did was narrow her eyes and mutter "Uh-huh," before grabbing the round of dough and rekneading Sue Anne's mess.

Sue Anne hustled over, her blue eyes animated. She grabbed my arm and steered me around the corner into the shadowed recess of the old wait station. "Billy James! Where have you been?"

I pulled my arm away. "What are you talking about? I was out listening to Cat like always." I fixed her with a glare. "And why would you wait in the kitchen to see me?"

She rolled her eyes. "Billy James, sometimes you are so dense it just boggles my mind. Didn't you see what happened tonight?"

What was she getting at? "Happened? Where?"

Sue Anne grabbed my shoulder and spun me toward the latticework that separated the wait station from the dining room. "Look. What do you see?"

I peered through the diamond-shaped holes. "The regulars. Eating. Drinking."

"In the center, doofus. The table in the center."

Then I knew what she meant. Preacher Cal. The incident with Mr. Williams. I turned, nearly banging my shoulder into her cheek. "What do you know about that?"

She grinned and crossed her arms. "Now you understand why I had to wait for you in the kitchen? We couldn't be seen talking together, now could we?"

The girl was certifiable. But she seemed to know something. "You know what Mr. Williams was so upset about?"

"Of course I do."

After a dramatic pause, I raised my brows. "Well? You gonna tell me or what?"

Sue Anne gave a satisfied "hmph," crossed her arms, and leaned in. "Seems Mr. Williams was made an offer today that he wouldn't accept. Preacher Cal and Mr. Finnegan were trying to talk him into taking it."

She frowned, and I was reminded of Gloria's nickname for Sue Anne. The bulldog. I swallowed a grin and peered out at Preacher Cal. "Okay, so what was the offer?" I knew it was wrong to gossip, especially with Sue Anne, but I had to know.

Sue Anne's breath was close to my neck. Her fingers latched onto the latticework as she stared out an adjoining gap. "It was Satan, of course."

She said his name like the biblical figure, even though she knew better. Fact was, just about everybody did, even though the real way of sayin' it was like "suntan" without the first "n."

"His hill's slippin' with all the rain. He wanted to hire Mr. Williams and Robby Peterson to shore it up. Buy all his supplies from the shop, pay up front, and everything."

That's what he'd come into town to do the day I went home early from school.

My mind buzzed around her words, and for a minute all I could see was Gloria grabbing ahold of Satan's hand that day in town. Doing what everyone warned us not to do.

"It makes perfect sense that Mr. Williams would say no," Sue Anne said.

But *why* did it make perfect sense? That's what I wanted to know, but I could tell from Sue Anne's face that she really didn't know either.

My fingers dug into the lattice. Even though Gloria spent time with Satan, she'd never said if she'd figured it out. I could still recall clear as day the Sunday she yanked me into the bell tower at church and told me she'd grabbed ahold of him in the alleyway over a month ago, and how she'd been hanging out with him ever since. I had gasped in shock, my insides all quivery, but her face was bright with an intense look—sort of overworked excitement mixed with a shine of rightness. It had left me feeling weird, disconnected, as if I wasn't sure who we were anymore.

"*He's wonderful, Billy . . . really wonderful . . . ,*" she'd said all spacey-like. And then she saw my face. It must have looked bad—horrified, maybe. All the excitement leeched out of her, and her mouth hardened like a stale block of cheese. "*You're just as scared as everyone else,*" she had spat as if it was some big surprise.

I don't remember what I said next, but she'd yelled, "*It's 'bout time to start taking control of your own life, Billy!*" before she ran out of the tower, her entire body stiff with offense, which made not a lick of sense. How had she expected me to react?

It was after that when things changed, when *she* started to change. First came the clothes. Instead of jeans and a T-shirt, she wore these funny long skirts, all black with coal-dark stockings. Then her hair, then the make-up. She was twelve! No one at school wore makeup.

She didn't talk to me much after that. Didn't show up at the tower at our regular times. Missed lots of school. Didn't come to church with her mama anymore. People started to talk. Was only natural that they would, but only I knew about Gloria's "secret friend." I was afraid to say anything, though. I knew Satan would be blamed for Gloria's sudden creepy transformation. And even though part of me blamed him, too, I knew Gloria would never talk to me again if I spilled the beans.

And then she brought over the box. It was bitter cold that day. An early spring freeze that made your face feel like it was on fire after only five minutes out of doors. I caught her up in the loft when I climbed the ladder, stuffing the box behind a bale of hay.

Her face was pale, her lips nearly blue. We locked eyes, and it didn't matter that she'd been acting like a lunatic for over a month. She was my best friend, uncertain and scared. It froze my insides, but I managed to shuffle over, my hands stuck under my armpits to hide their shaking.

There were no words for a while, just her and me shivering in the dim light of the loft, bits of moldy hay filtering through the frigid air. She pushed the box across the space between us. "Billy, I want you to hold on to this for me."

Some girls had a diary or a scrapbook. Gloria had the box. But it was more than a souvenir holder. I thought of it as a glimpse of who she was inside. That's why she hid it. Why she didn't share it with others, except me on occasion.

I didn't want it.

I looked at it like she was offering me a red-hot poker. "What? Why would I do that?"

"Because I'm asking you to."

"But why are you asking me to?"

Gloria was mum, which made everything stranger. After a sigh, she tucked the box behind the bale, then walked over to the ladder and pinned me with a fierce stare. Sharper than Gram's, more riveting than Mama's. I held my breath till my chest ached. "You don't go snoopin' in that unless something untoward happens to me, hear?"

I had no idea what "untoward" meant, but I nodded and watched as she shinnied down the ladder slick as you please.

Her feet thudded onto the hardpack below. I wanted to pop up and yell for her not to go. Beg her to tell me what was going on. What had Satan done to her? Why was she acting so different? But I didn't. I stood there saying nothing, doing nothing, like I didn't care, like it wasn't in me to care.

I listened to the measured swish as she walked to the door. A car honked outside. The barn door's rusted hinges creaked, and I knew she'd left.

*"You're as scared as everyone else!"* Her words rang in my ears.

"You look like you've seen a ghost, Billy James," said Sue Anne, all wide-eyed.

I stumbled around the corner and into the dining room. The sights and sounds filled my head: People eatin' and drinkin'. Some arguing. Some laughing. Servers rushin' to get orders. Preacher Cal holding audience at his table, arms wide as if calling his flock to order. Mr. Finnegan rubbing brink-bleary eyes. Mr. Williams's empty chair. . . .

Something shifted inside me, like our old tractor jerking from neutral into first gear.

"I'm *not* like them, Gloria. I'm not," I whispered.

# CHAPTER 10

**R**ay was home when we pulled up and got out of the car, along with Beavis and Tray. Empty beer cans littered the porch, some crushed, some still whole and leaking dribbles onto the deck.

A loud belch split the silence as we walked up. Laughter followed.

"Mama!" Ray unwound from his leggy slump and staggered forward.

Mama sighed. "Raymond Clay, you ain't supposed to be drinkin' . . . and aren't you supposed to be at work?"

Ray leaned heavily against the column and barked laughter. "That was before I decided Raymond Clay's made for better things than stacking lumber in some old reject's warehouse."

My eyes zoomed to Mama's face, which was pale. She let out an exhausted sigh and massaged her left arm like she had a cramp. "You mean you up and quit, Raymond Clay?"

Ray met Mama's eyes with a bold, confident stare. "That's right. Told Mr. Deacon I'd had a better offer. Something that would make use of my skills." He swung his arms wide and grinned. "Showcase my talent."

Tray and Beavis clapped and whistled. I kept looking at Mama. Was no way she'd fall for that. Not to mention, she had been the one to *get* Ray that job stacking and loading Copper Mill Paper Products. Jobs were hard to come by in Kelseyville. The lumber mill was about all there was for a fresh-from-school farm boy, and even then, getting in was like squeezing an apple through a square hole.

I licked my lips as a tiny thrill shot through me. Ray'd finally crossed the line.

"And what might that better offer be?" Mama asked, hand pressed to her chest.

Ray smiled and leaned forward, hands gripping the rail. "I'm gonna be a bounty hunter, Mama. Me, Beavis, and Tray. We're gonna catch bail jumpers, chase 'em down, then bring 'em to justice. Just like marshals in the Old West. Right, boys?" he shouted. A cheer went up, and my head nearly exploded.

Ray reached out and grabbed ahold of Mama's thick arm. "All I need, Mama, is the money to cover the test to get my license. After that I can start bringing in the felons and raking in the cash!" He mimicked a sniper pose, firing off two quick shots, before blowing on his barrel as Tray and Beavis fell dramatically to the deck, hands clutching their chests.

"Ya got me!"

"I'm at yer mercy!"

Was that a *smile* I saw on Mama's chapped lips? "All right, boys, drop the curtain. I've had a long night and I'm in no mood to watch your playactin'." She turned to Ray. "Clean up this mess, then come inside where we can discuss things proper."

Ray wrapped Mama in a hug and grinned a devil's

grin. "Yes, ma'am!" He pulled back and glared at Tray and Beavis. "You heard her. Pick up this mess!"

"That's the dumbest thing I ever heard!" I yelled.

All eyes fastened on me, like owls zeroing in on a mouse. "What'd you say?" whispered Ray. His red-rimmed gaze narrowed.

Heat rushed through me, and my mouth had a mind of its own. "I said that's the dumbest thing ever! No one's gonna hire you, let alone give you a gun, you big idiot!"

I saw Mama's palm a fraction of a second before it caught my face, sending a ringing into my ears. I stumbled backward, hand to my cheek.

Her eyes were glazed, almost fearful. "You apologize to your brother, Billy James," she whispered.

My heart fluttered wildly. She meant business, and as I looked at Ray, I knew I'd gotten off easy. Mama's slap was nothing compared to Ray's fist.

*Don't you apologize for the truth, Billy, never for the truth.*

I blocked out Gloria's voice and shuffled backward. "Sorry," I mumbled, before turning tail and running for the barn.

The hillside scents filled the air around my head as I trudged up the steep path after a late morning breakfast. My mind was *still* crowded with last night's events. I had slept in the loft, since Ray and Company J stayed the night. That letter was on my mind, and what Mr. Porter had said about my daddy. Did he know Ray Junior was following in our daddy's footsteps?

The only time I'd asked Ray about Daddy, he'd gone into a rage and made me promise never to ask again. Was six years with someone long enough to make a person just like them?

All the questions about tore me apart, so I'd started planning something drastic, something I had convinced myself to do after talking to Sue Anne. But all of a sudden, the plan seemed lame, suicidal even, as I forced myself through the ravine, past the crick, and up the side of Duard's Peak, my breath coming out in nervous little gasps.

I stopped and took a deep breath. This was the only way. Gloria hadn't told me about Satan, so I had to find out for myself. It was a sure bet no one in town was gonna tell me.

Shaking off my willies, I started to jog, the breeze cooling the sweat on the back of my neck. Clouds had moved in during the afternoon, and the air was heavy with ozone and the promise of rain. Trees grew denser the higher I went, and dark, mossy rocks jutted out of the hillside at odd angles. It looked a lot like Gram's hill, but thicker, and in a way, older.

Water tinkled nearby, and the sound eased the ragged nerves sounding off in my head. I turned off the dirt road and onto a deer trail that wound through shortleaf pines, and past a rocky outcrop covered with serviceberry and new blooming redbud. The trail would lead me somewhere near his place, since most of the hill homes were built close to the same things the whitetail deer frequented: water, dense cover, and a field wide enough to support summer grasses.

A loud crack sent me to my knees.

*Gunfire.*

It wasn't hunting season, but there were some who didn't

hold much with licenses and tags. If you heard a shot, you dropped and covered, then made as much human noise as possible and hoped they'd take a hint and light out.

Problem was, I didn't want to advertise my presence on Satan's hill.

Footsteps crashed through the bush, coming closer. I crouched. Sweat beaded on my forehead, as mold spores flew up my nostrils. I clapped a hand to my nose and pinched, my eyes bugging out.

There was no holding back. I fired off three sharp sneezes, trying to muffle them with my hand. More footsteps, and then—hooves! Black and shiny, they flashed by as a group of does and fawns zipped into the bracken on either side of me. Instinctively I covered my head and waited till they crashed their way down the hillside.

Sneezing again, I got to my knees and laughed. Not footsteps, but hoofsteps. Then I remembered the crack and ducked back down. "Crazy poachers," I mumbled.

"Not poaching. Helping."

*Satan.*

He towered over me, looking a lot like the scraggly pines. His coat rested against dark-clad legs nearly as tall as my shoulders.

I shot up. "Helping?" I squeaked.

He brought two polished sticks out in front of him and whacked them together, the crack reverberating through my chest like a twenty-two shot. I about messed myself right then and there.

Satan's eyes scanned the surrounding woods. "They come too close to the house. Dangerous for them to get comfortable around men."

My fingers clutched the nearest tree. *Run, Billy, run. . . .*

He stepped to the side, his large, thin body blocking the path. With pale fingers, he pushed the hat further down to hide his face, and I knew I didn't stand a chance if he wanted to grab me.

*This was a bad idea. . . .*

Thunder split the silence, and within seconds, rain started to fall. He looked up, then fastened his blue gaze on me. "You came to talk, yes?"

My throat was tight. All I wanted to do was go home. Even if Ray was there. Or Mama was mad. It didn't matter, as long as I wasn't here. With Satan.

*Prove it, Billy . . . prove it.*

Somehow I managed a nod, water dripping under my collar and onto my chest.

He sighed, then turned and waved a long-fingered hand. "Come. We'll talk over a cup of tea."

# CHAPTER 11

y the time we got to the cabin, we were both damp from the steady drizzle. Shrouded by fog and ringed by a thick stand of elms, Satan's cabin looked downright prehistoric. A shiver crept up into my calves, but I kept walking.

There was a small shack not far from the cabin with a rectangular corral attached to one side. Two marbled gray goats bleated from the paddock, their dark eyes following our trek across the clearing. I scanned everything that could use repair: steps, porch rail, chinks of missing caulk in the cabin walls . . . anything to keep my mind off of where I was and who I was with.

Satan stopped, and I nearly slammed into his back. I swallowed hard—and waited.

He bent over, all six and a half feet of him, and removed his boots, setting them on a woven rug beside the door. He motioned to my feet, too. I couldn't imagine what the big deal was, the way the outside of his cabin looked. Even so, I wasn't rude, so I pulled off my ragged, mud-flecked tennies and set them on the rug.

He motioned me inside, and fear crawled its way back into my belly.

My gaze rose. "Can—can we sit outside?"

Satan hesitated, but after a moment, he inclined his head toward the chairs. "Sit. I will bring tea."

He went inside, leaving the door open behind him. I sat. There was little furniture: a table with two chairs, a sofa off to one side, and shelves on the walls. My gaze wandered to the low rafters. Bunches of dried plants hung from strips of wire. Their spicy sweet scent wafted out the open door.

Lord Almighty, *I was at Mr. Satan's cabin!* Wouldn't Hog just spit if he knew. It was unbelievably weird. Surreal (another of Gloria's big words).

My eyes trailed Satan as he walked outside, an iron pot in one hand, two cups in the other.

Satan passed me and sat in the chair to my left before putting the cups and pot on the small table between us. As he poured, my eyes kept straying to his fingers. Both hands were long and bony with knotted knuckles, but while his movements with the right hand were smooth, almost dancelike, the left hand seemed jerky.

I swallowed thickly. No way I was drinking that tea.

He coughed and I looked up. He'd taken his hat off, and it was my first full-on view.

There was something wrong with his face.

It was slack on one side, like it was being pulled down toward his chin. I wondered why I hadn't noticed it before.

*The hats. The coats with the collar pulled all the way up to his ears.*

"Why do you come here?" he asked, his gaze curiously blank.

And his mouth . . . only one side of his lips moved when he spoke.

"Uh, well, I wanted to ask you . . ." I cleared my throat and dug for courage. *Think of Gloria, Billy. If she could do it, so can you.* "If maybe I could help you shore up the hillside?"

One eyebrow shot sky-high.

*Don't stop, Billy. Who cares what he looks like?* "I could do it, you know. I'm small, but strong. And with two of us working, we could reinforce the north side with a retaining wall before summer. There's some good granite over the rim. If we cut and pack it right, it'd take a mudslide the size of St. Louis to bring your cabin down."

"You want to help me?"

I nodded, my head on automatic pilot.

He wrapped his fingers around the delicate cup. His blue eyes fell onto my face, and the hairs on my arms stood on end.

"You could work up here several hours a week?"

I hadn't given much thought to the time involved. *Several hours a week with Satan.* "Y-yeah."

There was a pause, then, "Yes. I would welcome your help, Mr. Wilkins."

*Mr. Wilkins?*

My head snapped up. *How did he know my name?*

Fear made my lips tremble as I struggled for something to say.

He stared at me, the silence stretching between us

like a mile-long yardstick. Suddenly the cup in his hand started to shake, hot tea sloshing over his hand.

*Say something, Billy. Don't be a moron.* "I—I . . ."

Satan's leg thumped against the table, and my eyes zoomed to his face. He was white. A shade of white you didn't see on a body. Unless they were dead.

I jumped up, the chair striking the railing behind me. "What's wrong?"

As quickly as the bizarre shaking started, it stopped. Satan collapsed forward onto the table, his hands splayed across the knotted wood. With his head still hung low, he murmured, "You go now."

I stood frozen, my heart thumping so hard it near choked me.

He lurched to his feet. "GO!"

I fumbled backward, leapt the steps two at a time, and ran. My bare feet sliced into the damp mountain earth like the black hooves that had gone before.

I tossed the comic aside.

It was no use. Nothing was gonna keep my mind from thinking about what happened at Satan's an hour before.

My gaze fastened on the sky outside the open loft door. Clouds peppered the robin's egg blue, and I breathed deep, damp filling my lungs.

I couldn't believe that I'd run out on Satan like a headless, and shoeless, chicken. What if he needed help? A doctor, or medicine. I shuddered, and sunk deeper into the hay.

Satan definitely didn't make sense.

The way he looked. The way he acted and sounded. All weird. All different and unexplainable.

And how had he known my name?

Had Gloria mentioned me?

I covered my face with both arms. *What if Satan had something contagious?* Was that why we were told not to touch him? Was it possible that he had infected Gloria with something?

*Could it possibly be that simple?*

Nothing was ever that simple. Just like learning about Micah Porter. I hadn't given much thought to Daddy for years now. Until that letter. And now thoughts of him kept popping up. Questions. What was it like at home with Daddy before I came along? And most important, why'd he leave?

"Uh, hello? Are you in here?"

Startled, I scrambled to the loft edge and sucked in a breath when I spotted Gloria's little brother by the barn door. *What is he doing here?* "Hey," I called down.

He walked inside and squinted up. "I want to talk to you."

The perfect ending to a perfectly horrible day. "You want to talk, you'll have to come up," I said, figuring Palm Springs would chicken out and leave me in peace. Instead, he scrunched up his face and grabbed hold of the ladder.

Scooting over, I held fast to the rickety wood. All I needed was for him to fall and break his neck.

After a lot of grunting, his flushed face came into view, and he crawled into the loft.

"How'd you know where to find me?" I asked, none too friendly.

He stood all awkward and shrugged. "It wasn't that hard."

I snorted.

His hands knotted on his hips. "Okay, okay. I asked this stupid girl who's been coming over to the house about you. She said to follow Starling Road to the white-and-blue-trimmed house with a big old barn out front. When I knocked, your mom said you were probably out here."

I tried not to look at the familiar shape of his eyes, or the stubborn set to his chin. "Why were you looking for me?"

He was quiet for a minute, chewing his lower lip. His eyes flicked to mine, a deep question brewing there. "I had something to ask you."

"Fire away."

"You knew my sister," he blurted. It was a statement, not a question, and my belly tightened.

"Everyone in town did."

He sat across from me. "No, I mean you *really* knew her. You were like best friends, right?"

I was quiet for a minute, wondering where his questions were coming from.

He poked out his lower lip and jumped up. "You're just like everyone else here! No one wants to talk about her. It's like she never existed!"

My heart withered like a summer apple in dead winter. I reached out and grabbed his arm. "Wait!"

After a moment, he sat stiffly, and my head spun as I tried to sort out my feelings and thoughts. "We—we were good friends."

He looked away, hugging himself tight. "Tell me what she was like."

I sighed. He needed something real to chew on. "She was great. Smart, really smart, and. . ." Gloria popped to life in my mind fully formed, her wry smile shining down on me. "Funny. She made me laugh."

His eyes lit up. "Did she tell jokes?"

"Yeah. And she sang these God-awful songs that drove me crackers." The tightness in my chest faded. "All sad and moody. But she had a good voice, smooth like one of my mama's sugar cream pies."

"A what?" he asked, his stubby nose wrinkling.

"You've never had sugar cream pie?"

"Uh-uh. Is it sweet?"

"Yep. 'Cause that's all it is. Sugar, cream, and egg yolks."

He licked his lips, and I found myself grinning. "Hey, I still don't know your name."

"Why not?"

Good question. "Well, Gloria never told me what it was."

His eyes widened. "Really? That's weird. It's Nicholas. Nick, for short."

"How'd you know me and Gloria were friends?"

He rolled his eyes. "That girl. She kept coming over and asking me all these questions. So I asked her some right back."

"Was this girl named Sue Anne?"

"Yeah! That's it. She keeps bringing food over. My mo—Delilah, wasn't very happy about it." He shrugged. "Not that I care if she's happy or not."

"So you came to ask about Gloria?"

He nodded solemnly, his fingers brushing at dust on his jeans.

"What about your mama? Hasn't she told you about your sister?"

"She says the same thing over and over again whenever I ask. 'My poor little Gloria, taken by God before her time.'" He frowned. "Then she says she wants us to make a new start, like she wants to forget all about my sister!"

A thick sadness crept over me as I thought of all the bad feelings weighing on so many people. "Well, it sounds like your mama's still grieving hard."

We were quiet for a moment, listening to the soft tick, tick of the breeze teasing at the barn door.

"Was she—did Gloria do something bad? Is that why no one wants to talk about her?"

Satan sprung into my head. "No! No, she didn't do anything bad." *How to explain?* "She was different than a lot of the folks here. People don't take kindly to folks who are different."

Nick's brow wrinkled. "Well, that's stupid!"

"Yeah, it is. Real stupid." Heat rushed into my face. Lord, Gloria was right. I *was* as bad as everyone else in Kelseyville, running out on Satan like that. He did tell me to leave, but I could have refused. Tried to help him. It's no wonder Gloria wouldn't talk to me about Satan. Why she went about things on her own.

"Your sister spoke her mind and did right by people, staying true to herself at the same time." I chewed the fresh skin on my lower lip where the scab had fallen off, and my eyes watered from the sting. "Do you know what that means, staying true to yourself?"

Nick puckered his lips to one side, then gazed at me all serious. "Uh, she did what she thought was right? Even if other people didn't agree?"

I closed my eyes. "Yeah. That's it exactly."

"I didn't want to come here, you know." Tension climbed in Nick's voice. "I didn't think I should have to when she didn't have an interest in knowing about me. But he made me, my dad. He said it was the right thing to do."

I opened my eyes and looked at Nick, his fists tight in his lap. "Your daddy was right, Nick. It wasn't Gloria's fault she died, and I'm sure she would want you to spend time with your mama and—"

Nick popped up, hands knotted at his sides. "How would *you* know? You didn't even know about me. Gloria didn't care if *I* existed. Why should I care now that *she's* dead?"

"Now, hold on." I reached for his arm, but he darted over to the ladder.

"I don't know why I came to talk to *you*. Like she would have been best friends with some grungy hill-billy!" With that he climbed down as fast as his pudgy body would allow.

"Be careful on your way home and stay on the road" was all I managed to call down as he hit the floor and ran out the door without a backward glance.

# CHAPTER 12

etting time away from the house turned out to be as easy as pulling dandelions after a hard rain. Without a job, Ray'd lost his apartment and moved back home, so being gone as much as possible was a given. And Mama seemed mighty distracted anyway. She was probably worrying about Ray's stupid plan to take that test in Windell, and how she was gonna get the money to pay for it.

Ray'd actually brought home a book to study, but books and Ray were like cows and ragweed, likely to lead to explosive ends when mixed together. I remembered clear as day how crazy Ray used to get when he had homework to do. Before he even cracked a book, he'd holler and thrash around like our old coon dog Sunshine when she had a burr in her ear. All the time Mama'd stand over him with that wooden spoon threatening to whack him good if he didn't get busy.

"By God, my sons are getting an education!" she used to say, spoon held high like the Statue of Liberty's torch. I could never figure why Ray thwarted her on that point—until later. In high school the teachers told us that they thought Ray was dyslexic. After that Mama stopped raising the spoon and started paying for Ray to go to some special classes so he could graduate, and he did. I figured Ray made up some of his trouble for attention. But who knows. Either way, I couldn't help but think he was cooking something up by bringing the book home. Maybe trying to figure a way to get more money out of Mama.

At least it was easy to go my own way without Ray or Mama payin' much notice—especially given where I was headed now. I followed the same deer trail, muddy and rutted from the recent rain. After talking to Nick, it felt more important than ever to figure out why Gloria had spent so much time with Satan. And there was only one person still alive who could tell me that.

I wiggled my toes in Ray's old shoes and tried to ignore the gaping holes. At least my feet didn't feel squished. What a doofus I was for running off without my shoes.

The question was, would Satan still want my help?

And more important, could I give him that help without freezin' up and actin' a fool?

Satan's cabin looked small and unimportant in the rain-slicked meadow. Smoke curled out of the chimney, and he stood on the front stoop, head bowed over something.

I took a deep breath, crossed the clearing, and stopped a few feet from the steps. Satan's head rose, a look of tranquil unconcern on his face. Panic pricked me, but I wasn't going to give in to it. No matter what.

He blinked a few times before inclining his head. "Mr. Wilkins."

Swallowing the lump in my throat, I nodded back. "Mr. Satan."

My gaze eased to the chunk of wood in his hand. His other held a short knife. "You whittle?" I asked.

He nodded, then went back to what he was doing. His hands flew over the shapeless mass, taking off a chunk here, a shave there. In fifteen minutes, it went from hunk of lumber to snarling wolf.

My hands itched just to see it, and I knew I was witnessing an amazing talent. Like a concert pianist, or Olympic athlete.

When Satan was done, he rubbed the wolf with a cloth, buffing the wood a rich, smoky brown. He handed it to me and I took it, making sure our hands didn't touch. I turned the wolf over, noting every fine ridge, the strength of its legs, the depth of its chest. "It's unbelievable," I said, forgetting all about my hesitation.

"It is for you," Satan said.

I sat the wolf respectfully on the steps. "Thanks, but I can't accept it."

Satan was silent for a moment, then stood. He picked something up near the door and brought it to me.

My shoes!

He placed them by my feet. "These you can take."

Something shivered deep inside my chest. My Keds were shiny clean, not a trace of mud. Dry, too. And as I turned them over, I realized the sole had been glued back down and the hole near the toe had been seamlessly mended.

While Satan's face was as droopy and somber as ever, I could have swore part of him was smiling. "Thanks," I said.

Without a word, Satan walked down the steps and disappeared in the shed across from his cabin. I waited, wondering what he was up to, and whether to follow him or stay put.

In a matter of minutes, he emerged with an old mule hooked up to a handmade sledge. Behind him came the two goats, tails flicking. The darker goat bleated a greeting then trotted up, giving me an animal appraisal. Guess I must've passed inspection, because it bobbed its head in my direction, then bleated a second time.

With Satan leading, we trudged into the woods.

*Should I apologize for runnin' out?*

Our silence seemed fitting, so I kept my mouth shut and studied the woods instead. They were thicker this side of Duard's Peak. Hickory blended with heavy clusters of oak, blocking out much of the light and littering the ground with a layer of damp leaves.

The mule plodded along like she'd done it hundreds of times. We were climbing steadily, but not in the direction of the granite crag where I'd assumed we'd get the stone. After a few more minutes, we stopped in an area so thick with new timber, it would have been hard for even skinny me to get through without turning sideways.

Gram's voice erupted in my head. *Always know how to git back to where you started in these woods, Billy.*

Satan began unloading the sledge.

I watched, wanting to help but knowing it would put me tight to Satan in a too close spot. Just then a sneeze hit me like a thresher on steroids.

"God bless," said Satan.

I stared at him in surprise. "Thanks."

It had never occurred to me that Satan might be a religious man. But then, "God bless" was as common as "bless you." And what did it matter? That's what Gloria would've said.

Preacher Cal would think it mattered. So would most everyone else in town.

"Are—are you leaving the tools here?" I asked, scratching my head.

He straightened and assessed me with those cool blue eyes. "We cannot build the wall with stone. Not without more help. Equipment."

My mouth got worked up to disagree, but I stopped and thought for a minute. Ray and I had built small retaining walls, but on larger ones workers used big tractors to haul boulders for the base, then stacked the more manageable rock from there.

I eyed the mottled gray mule.

There was no way we'd be able to make that happen, let alone leverage the stones in place. Not with my scrawny arms and Satan's twisted-up—

It wasn't proper, thinking that way. Gram would have been the first one to give me "the look," no explanation needed.

As I stared at the trees, my mind filled with images of the mud that we'd need to hold back to save Satan's cabin. Trees and their deep-rooted fingers are what naturally hold the soil onto the hillsides. But we couldn't plant trees to stand against the pour-downs sure to come.

I pictured Satan's cabin and worried my lower lip all over again.

That's when it hit me.

"A wall of wood," I whispered.

"Yes. We will borrow from the forest to save the knoll," said Satan as he moseyed up to a young oak and placed a hand on the rough bark.

Well, there was plenty of wood. It wouldn't be pressure treated, something important for lumber exposed to the elements. I said as much, and Satan nodded. "But there is no alternative. It will likely last long enough."

*Long enough for what?* I wanted to ask, but didn't.

A funny sensation settled in my chest at his words. I went over to get a better look at the tools. There were chisels and wedges of various sizes. Old ones, the metal darkened with age, but clean, their edges sharp-looking. A mallet and sledge hammer. Two different types of handsaws, an old auger-type drill, and an impressive axe. I ran a finger over its polished wood handle. It was decorated with what looked like deer antlers and leaves.

Satan reached over my head for the axe.

I yanked my hand away and stumbled backward. My face burned but he seemed not to notice as he hefted the tool and gazed at it fondly, blocking my only exit. "Granddad carved the handle," he murmured. "The wood was kind to him."

*The wood was* kind *to him? What did* that *mean?*

I scooted to the back of the sledge, my hands pressed against the splintery wood, my eyes stuck on the axe. "Your family, are they all out of the country?" I ventured.

Satan held the axe and eyed the trees. "Yes."

"Where are they? What country?"

"Now the Czech Republic," Satan answered. "And some in Bulgaria." He reached out and touched a few of the trees, then moved on to the next group.

"Did you ever live there?" I moved a few more inches away. Then a couple of feet.

Satan nodded. "When I was a baby, then again as a young man."

It was hard to picture Satan as a baby. I wondered if he was born with the droopiness in his face. Gerald Simmons at school was born with a short arm. From shoulder to elbow it looked okay, but his hand hung only inches away from the joint. Gerald could do a lot with that short arm, so it wasn't as if anyone really thought of him as crippled.

I edged my way to the far side of the narrow glade. "What was it like there?"

Satan sighed, his gaze still focused on the trees. "I do not remember much from when I was very young. But when I was there as a man, it was a beautiful country. The woods where my family came from were like this—rich, full. There was much water." He smiled crookedly. "Good fishing."

I was trying to picture it in my head, but all I could think on was why Satan had placed a hand on one particular oak, then closed his eyes. In the following silence, the questions knotted in my throat like a tangled ball of yarn.

Finally he smiled softly and opened his eyes. "This one. We start here."

Satan stepped back and raised the axe.

I jumped nearly a coon's length, my heart slamming against my rib cage.

The tree. He was going to chop down the tree he'd been touching.

His swing was sure, and the blade thunked solidly into the oak.

My breath fell out in one heavy sigh, but Satan didn't seem to notice. He went right back to his task.

The sound of even chopping filled the woods.

We spent the remainder of my two hours on the hill cutting down trees. As soon as one fell, I grabbed the handsaw and went to work. I cut each log into six-foot lengths at Satan's request, and piled the debris in a far corner of the glade. Sawing by hand was hard work, and before long my arms felt as if there were burning coals buried in my muscles. But Satan didn't stop, so I kept sawing, surprised at the easy rhythm we'd fallen into.

The goats, which were named Gertie and Gustav, hung around like faithful hounds. They yanked leaves off trees and bleated every so often. Satan raised his head each time they did, as if he might be expecting someone. It was unnerving, and pretty soon I was looking, too.

I wasn't sure *what* we were looking out for. Hunters, maybe. Or bears. Blackies still roamed our mountains. Hounds were the best way to drive them away, but goats could at least warn you before a bear stumbled onto a body.

As the sun eased itself westward, Satan called a halt to the cutting. Relief washed through me. My day with Satan was finally nearing its end.

Together we bound the logs and loaded them onto the cart. Penny the mule gazed at us with dark, knowing eyes as the cart jiggled and settled across her shoulders and flank. With Satan leading the mule downhill, we exited the woods at the base of the granite knoll, then followed a well-worn path.

"I wonder how long we have until the next big storm," I said, gazing skyward.

"Some time," Satan responded matter-of-factly. "Light rain will come, but it will be two weeks before the heavy ones arrive."

How could he be so positive? I studied him as we walked. His gait was a bit crooked, but his steps were sure. He'd at least shed his coat while we worked. It was draped over the tools in the cart, and I couldn't help but notice Satan wasn't as old as I'd figured. He had muscle beneath that stick-thin exterior, and after witnessing him hauling and working, I guessed he had to be closer to Mama's age than Gram's.

Which meant that Satan must've gone to school in Kelseyville. I couldn't imagine that.

We rounded the last corner and stood beneath the southern rim of Satan's hill. Mud and chert tracked down the slope in bits and chunks, and it was obvious where the trouble had started. A knotty pine jutted out from the right side of the rise, and with the rains, a sizable boulder had tumbled loose from its roots, exposing the underbelly of the hillside. A retaining wall probably should have been built when the cabin was first erected, but if Satan's daddy's resources were anything like Satan's, it was a pure wonder the cabin got built at all.

We rolled the logs out of the cart, and Satan explained what he planned to do. Our first tasks would be cutting and shaping the wood and digging footings and a trench for the crossbeams. The plan was sound, but I wondered how Satan figured to do it with outdated hand tools and no concrete.

I scratched my head and tried to come up with a way to ask him about the supplies without mentioning Mr. Williams. Just thinking about the store owner had me feeling flush with guilt. "Uh, well, the timbers will probably work, but, uh, what about bolts? And concrete?"

Satan leaned on the axe handle and sighed. He looked plumb worn-out, his face droopy as ever.

What if he *did* have some terrible disease? Or worse?

The back of my neck went cold.

*Don't think like that, Billy. . . .*

I took a deep breath, then sat on the edge of the sledge. I could probably buy those things for Satan, but the question was, would he want me to after Mr. Williams had turned him down?

"We'll need those things," I said. "Right?"

Satan looked like he was thinking it over. His eyes were painfully blue in the afternoon sun, his light brown hair curling slightly over his ears. He looked sort of regal, standing there, like someone you saw in a painting or old photograph. "Maybe not, Mr. Wilkins. Maybe there is a way to do without."

I didn't see how, but maybe he knew something I didn't. Either way, it was going to be that much harder without them, even if there *was* a way.

An unexpected knot of determination looped in my

chest, and I knew I was gonna get those supplies. I wasn't sure why or how, but I was certain I would.

Satan gave me a measured look. "Do not worry. We will make do."

I imitated his nod while pulling my shoelaces out of Gertie's mouth and thinking up a way to make it happen.

# CHAPTER 13

eaning against the splintered back of our porch swing, I blinked up into the sinking afternoon sun. My body felt strangely relaxed, and even the ache in my shoulders was sorta pleasant. Like something well earned.

Who would've thought three weeks ago I'd be working side by side with Satan?

Mama's shoes clumped on our hardwood kitchen floor, and the screen door banged open.

She had her workbag over one shoulder and two large covered trays in her hands. "Billy James, you stay close to home, hear? I'll be back near ten."

"Okay." I jumped up and ran over to open the door of the Dodge. She hustled down the steps and into the car. Sometimes I wondered how she ever got all the ordinary stuff done around the house with her baking for the diner and all. Seemed like the oven was lit and roasting seven days a week.

I waved as she pulled out onto the limestone drive. I'd told Mama I didn't feel up to going to Greystokes tonight. Truth was, the thought of seeing Sue Anne,

Preacher Cal, or even Cat turned my stomach. I wanted more than anything to tell Cat about my helping Satan. He'd probably be the only one who would understand, but it wasn't worth the risk.

What if he didn't understand? I shivered. I wasn't sure exactly what would happen . . . but it couldn't lead to anything good.

Rubbing my bare feet, I stared out across our yard toward Gram's hill.

Despite all the things shouting for space in my thick head, my thoughts drifted back to my daddy. How could I find out more about him, short of asking Micah Porter?

Asking Mama directly would be pure foolishness.

Gram was a possibility, but she'd probably just say it was Mama's piece to speak or keep quiet as she saw fit.

So that left Ray.

Yeah, right. It wasn't a good day to die.

I thought hard on all the things Mama had said about Daddy: that he left of his own accord, not because she made him, and that he'd gone to meet his maker not long after, and that he was a man with demons riding him every moment of his life.

And those tidbits of information hadn't come all at once, either.

The house and yard were dead quiet after the car fumed its way down the road. There weren't even any crickets chirping, which gave me the willies. I quit the porch swing and went up to my room.

Moving my quilt aside, I pulled Gloria's box out from under the bed. It was ugly and unappealing again, now that the flaps were glued. Something Mama'd probably throw away if she found it, thinking it was an old piece of junk.

But it wasn't junk. I shook it gently. It barely made a sound, but it was heavy.

*Open it.*

It wasn't Gloria's voice in my head. It was mine, but I wasn't about to listen. I shoved the box to the very back of the bed near the wall and lowered my quilt. Not yet. My mouth was firecracker dry.

The box got me to thinking, though. If Gloria kept things she didn't want anyone to see but her, maybe other girls—women—did, too. Maybe someone like my Mama.

The next day I hit Satan's knob thirty minutes after school let out. Mama was busy whipping up a new pie for the diner, and Ray was nowhere to be found—as usual.

Satan and I had more cutting to do, but I'd come prepared this time. I had a pair of my old leather gloves tucked into my back pocket. Had to have something to cover the molehill-size blisters on my palms from the dang saw. I figured the gloves afforded me some protection from Satan, too, should he get the idea in his head to grab me with one of those bony hands.

He was out front feeding the animals when I walked up. Chickens scrabbled at scraps around the fenced garden, while the goats munched grain from their trough. He nodded politely in my direction before going into the shed with his buckets. I stood there, hands locked behind my back, my eyes strayin' across everything in sight. Satan's glade was a pretty one. Bigger than Gram's, and wilder. Flowers were already popping up along the edges and in the small gullies where the rainwater traveled and the grass thickened.

I wasn't sure what Satan was doing in the shed, so I walked the clearing. Chunks of rock peeked through the dark earth in spots. I stopped at Satan's garden. It was thick with overwintered woody herbs. Fresh seedlings were just popping their way through the dirt in several neat rows. I took a handful of soil, squeezing. Since it held together some, Satan must have spent time enriching the normally hardscrabble earth.

"It has taken time to build the soil."

Satan's voice nearly sent me headfirst into the chicken mesh. I sidled over, looking up into his pale face. "You—you use manure?" I asked.

Satan waved a hand and led me to the rear of the shed. Four piles of compost sat steaming. I recognized them all. Chicken manure. Goat manure. And a final mixture that probably combined both with other organic waste. The fourth was the completed pile. I picked up a handful and ran my fingers through its earthy grains. It was rich, fine. A perfect additive for the rocky hillside soil.

"Come." Satan walked off into the larger part of the shed. The outside might have looked weathered, but inside was neat as a pin and warm. Fresh hay sat stacked on the far wall, and Penny stood placidly chewing over her trough in a separate stall. I spotted the sledge near the hay and went to bring it over as Satan led Penny out. We had her hooked up in just a few minutes.

"We cut more today," Satan said as we made our way up the narrow path to our logging site.

I pulled my gloves out of my pocket. There were small holes along the knuckles and down a couple of the seams, but that was okay. Mama had promised me new ones next winter, as she said my hands would have outgrown the holes by then anyhow.

We set right to work once we got there. Satan picked which tree to fell, and I watched him carefully each time. He did that peculiar thing, where he'd stare at the tree for a minute, then place his hand square in the middle and close his eyes.

Sometimes he moved on to another before cutting. Part of me wanted to know what he was doing and why. Another part was afraid to know.

At least he'd taken the time to give me a couple of pointers when it came to shaping up the logs, then moved aside and let me get on with it. He didn't criticize or correct me at every turn.

By the end of day two, we'd chopped and shaped near to twenty logs. The area we'd worked looked thinner, but in a way that made you see the real possibility of a space. Like cutting out an overgrown patch of ragweed in a yard.

We dropped the lumber off near the knoll, then headed back to the cabin. As we went to unhook Penny, I noticed that Satan's hands were shaking, his arm dangling at an odd angle. A tickle of unease hit my insides. "Here," I said, reaching for the harness. "I'll take care of it."

Satan paused, as if getting ready to say no, but instead he straightened and nodded. "Yes. Thank you."

I got the mule unhooked and back into her paddock in no time. "So, I guess I'll be back tomorrow," I said, checking him out while trying to look casual.

Satan's arms stayed limp at his sides and his face was slightly gray, but his gaze was firm. "Thank you again, Mr. Wilkins. Your help has been invaluable."

It was my turn to nod, and since more words seemed a waste, I headed downhill toward home.

# CHAPTER 14

It was hard to believe Saturday was already here. Mama had gotten real fussy about things at the house, and I'd only gotten to Satan's two days out of the entire week.

Mama'd always liked things clean, but repainting the garage was getting out of hand. Neither Ray nor I could figure out what had gotten into her, but we did as she said.

I almost got up the guts to ask Ray about Daddy while we worked. But it just didn't seem worth the possible repercussions. Besides, I had other things to think about, like how I was going to get the concrete and lag bolts for Satan's wall.

As soon as Ray left with Company J, I told Mama I was going into town to pick up weed killer and manure for the vegetable garden. That way it wouldn't look too strange me walkin' into town with a wheelbarrow. We had an account at Mr. Williams's store, but I'd also emptied my money jar so I could buy the concrete and bolts. Nineteen-fifty wasn't much, but it was all I had.

*Wait a minute.* No it wasn't.

I bolted to the laundry hamper. Digging through

over a week's worth of clothes, I finally hit bottom and pulled out the shirt I'd worn to Greystokes the night Preacher Cal had driven off Mr. Williams.

"Yes," I whispered, reaching inside the pocket. The four dollars Preacher Cal had forced me to take. Now I had twenty-four-fifty.

As the wheelbarrow bounced its way down the road, I kept thinking about Satan. The more time I spent with him, the more I realized how complicated he was. He didn't talk much, and when he did, it was just simple statements. Sometimes he sounded a lot like Cat and Gloria, but unlike them, Satan didn't do any explainin' when he saw my look of bewilderment.

Also, he never once tried to touch me. Which was okay, as my body still flinched at the thought of him laying those long-fingered hands on me.

The only thing I didn't find strange was Satan staying up on his hillside. Gram had done the same, and there was nothing wrong in *her* head. And while I hadn't seen any more of Satan's carvings, I wanted to. I couldn't get over how well his hands worked when he was holding that knife. How fine his carvings were.

It was almost magical.

Thinking about Satan left me shivery inside, as if someone could look right at me and know who I'd been helping. As I crossed the street to Mr. Williams's shop, my head felt loaded with cotton. *It's no big deal. Mr. Williams won't know I'm buyin' supplies for Satan.*

I left the wheelbarrow outside and opened the glass-paned door. The bell jingled, and I stepped inside.

"Well, hi there, Billy James."

Mrs. Williams stood behind the counter in her apple-green apron that read "Williams Hardware, Labor and Supply. We Aim to Please" in bold red letters across the front. She smiled, and I smiled back, feeling as if there were a sock lodged behind my rib cage.

"Uh, I'm here to pick up some weed killer. For the dandelions."

There, that hadn't been so bad.

Mrs. Williams pointed to the shelves at the back of the store. "Sure thing. Pick the one you want and we'll ring you up."

I searched the shelves she'd pointed to. There were about a bazillion products that claimed to kill, wipe out, or "vegetize" just about anything living. I grabbed the cheapest one, then went to the rear of the store where the construction stuff was kept.

Plaster . . . sand . . . woodchips . . . *Aha,* concrete. The bags were big. I could barely lift one an inch off the floor.

"You need some help, son?"

Mr. Williams was standing over me like a bear on two legs. "Uh, well, I . . ."

His eyebrows rose. "Son, you aren't going to be able to lift those on your own." He looked around. "You got a cart?"

"No. I'll get one." I hurried to the front, grabbed the shopping cart, and zoomed back to the rear of the store. "I need, uh, three bags, please."

He nodded, muscles bulging as he lifted. Little puffs of gray dust squirted out as each bag dropped into the cart.

"What're you fixin' to work on?"

My heart dropped into my toes. *Lie, Billy, lie . . .*

"Ray and I are building a special raised flower bed for Mama."

He smiled, and I felt like kicking myself. *Why had I involved Ray?*

"And you need three bags for that?"

I nodded but kept silent.

After a pause . . . "Well, that's right fine of you boys. Good to see brothers working together." He frowned and the muscles in his neck corded. He cleared his throat and turned the cart. "Yep. A nice thing to do. You'll need some wood preservative, too, you plannin' on putting posts in concrete. You have lumber already?"

I figured he might ask about the lumber, so I had a response all worked out. "We have a stack of beams in the shed left over from some other project that never got done."

Mr. Williams nodded and took a silver can off a shelf and added it to the cart. "This will keep your posts from rotting. Your mama waiting out front in the car? I'll load up for you."

"Well, it's kind of a surprise, so I'm going to take them back in my wheelbarrow. It's out front."

Mr. Williams's bushy eyebrows went up again.

I knew he was looking at my scrawny arms and wondering how I'd ever get the concrete home. I straightened. "I've pushed heavier stuff."

Shaking his head, Mr. Williams wheeled the cart up front. "Guess I'll have to take your word for it."

"Oh, wait!" The bolts! "I, uh, also need some bolts. To hold everything together."

Mr. Williams paused and cocked his head to one

side. "Bolts, huh? Well, we got lots of those. Come on." He led me over two aisles, stopping at a long bank of wooden troughs. They were filled to the brim with every imaginable bolt, nut, and screw.

"What size do you need, son?"

Sweat beaded on my neck and slipped between my shoulder blades. "Well, we're using pretty thick beams. Five inches, I think Ray said."

*There I go involving Ray again.*

Mr. Williams went right to them. "About like this?" He held one up. Light glinted off the bright silver.

"Yeah. That looks right." I searched for the price.

A dollar apiece! That was way more than I'd figured. And we'd need about ten. I swallowed—hard.

Mr. Williams grabbed a small paper bag. "How many, Billy?"

"Uh, about ten." My voice cracked as I tried to add everything up in my head.

It would be real close to my twenty-four dollars. Back at the register, Mr. Williams ruffled my hair. "Candy, give young Mr. Wilkins a ten percent discount on account he's so good to his mama." He smiled, and I felt guiltier than ever. Guilty for lying. Guilty for using his stuff to do something I knew he was dead-set against.

Mrs. Williams's fingers flew on the register keys. "We've always known Billy was a fine, upstanding boy." Mrs. Williams gave me another bright smile. "With the discount it comes to twenty-three fifty-seven."

Just enough. I didn't even need to put the weed killer on Mama's credit.

I handed over my twenty-four dollars. "You take care now, Billy," Mrs. Williams said.

"Thanks." I flicked a quick glance at Mr. Williams, who'd moved to the front door with my cart.

Outside, Mr. Williams loaded my purchases into the wheelbarrow. "Awful lot to be pushing home. Sure you don't want to call someone?"

I shook my head, slipped on my gloves, and lifted the handles. My legs and back strained with the weight. Pushing it was going to be another matter altogether.

Mr. Williams gave the wheelbarrow a quick shove to get me moving. "Good luck, son."

"Right," I said again, pushing for all I was worth and wishing old Penny was around to help.

I leaned against the wheelbarrow and stared up at Satan's hill, my entire body screaming with weariness. There was no way the wheelbarrow was gonna move another inch. Not under Billy power, anyway.

But I'd done it. Gotten Satan the supplies he needed (well, at least the ones we couldn't do without), and Mr. Williams didn't suspect a thing.

The thought gave me a wobbly sense of satisfaction, but just as quickly, a keen sense of dread straightened me right up.

There had to be some logical reason why Mr. Williams felt so all-fire hateful toward Satan. Mr. Williams wasn't a bad guy. Maybe not the easy-laughing type, but nice enough. And so was Mrs. Williams. What would inspire them to hate a man so?

I brushed off my palms, picked up the bolts and

preservative, then left the wheelbarrow and made my way toward the path that led up to Satan's hill. No need to worry about someone tripping over it. Satan's road wasn't even graded and re-rocked at the end of each winter like it should have been. The chance that it would see traffic in the next hour was about as likely as parts arriving a day early for a broken-down car.

Ten yards in I heard the bleating.

Gertie.

She tip-tapped around the bend, her bushy tail twitching, and stopped when she saw me. Gustav joined her, his liquid black eyes staring at me unblinking. Satan followed with Penny and the cart.

Satan pulled up alongside. "Mr. Wilkins," he said, inclining his fedora-topped head like he'd been expecting me.

"Mr. Satan," I said, my chest near to bursting with the sudden lack of air. "What're you doing here?"

Satan looked at the wheelbarrow sitting in the center of the lane. "You need help, no?"

My mouth went bone-dry. "Uh, yeah. But how'd you know?"

Satan didn't respond. Instead, he urged Penny next to the wheelbarrow and started to unpack it. I went to help him.

Between the two of us, we managed to get the concrete bags loaded without too much of a problem. Satan was quiet the entire time, and I couldn't tell if he was mad about me getting the supplies. But the bigger question was *how* Satan knew I would buy them, and even if he'd guessed I would, how he knew when I'd be bringing them. All sorts of ideas ran wild through my mind.

Satan reached into his back pocket and pulled out a wallet. "What do I owe you, Mr. Wilkins?"

Owe me?

I waved a hand and shook my head.

He fixed me with a no-nonsense stare. Almost as firm as Gram's, which made my head feel funny. Like maybe I'd been underestimating Satan this whole time. "The price, please."

I did some quick calculations. "Uh, about twenty dollars."

Three twenties appeared between his fingers and he held them out. "You take this. There will be more for the work you are doing. Ten dollars an hour, a fair wage."

My hands remained stuck to my sides. *He's paying me?* I opened my mouth to protest, but that look in his eye stopped me. I reached out and took the money without touching his fingers.

"Uh, thanks. I'll give you the receipt, and ten dollars an hour is, well a lot. More than I need, really. How about eight?"

Satan's stern expression halted my tongue. "Mr. Wilkins, never underestimate your worth."

He got Penny moving back in the other direction, and I followed behind, the money tucked into my back pocket.

# CHAPTER 15

"Work is like prayer," Satan told me as we dug our postholes. "Pure focus of mind and spirit on one principle." He pointed to the depression in the soil. "To dig, or to chop. Or lift." He wiped his brow and sighed as a sudden breeze teased our skin. "One task, then another. Give each your full attention."

While I rammed my posthole digger in and out of the rocky soil, I thought about his words. It was true. . . . I could do that. Get so wrapped up in a task it was all that existed in my mind for that moment. Like when I was fixin' things. But prayer?

When I had prayed before Gloria died, there were always a million other things running through my head. School. Ray. Mama or one of our sick animals. And then there were the other people in church whisperin' and praisin' and shifting in their tight pews and too small Sunday pants and dresses.

I pushed hair off my forehead, leaned on the shovel, and appraised our work. We'd done pretty darn well in only three hours.

Satan plunked his shovel into the soil and walked

over to a rough bench he'd fashioned out of our scraps. I joined him, keeping a safe distance between us, my arms and calves aching.

He brought out a jug and two cups, and as we sat he poured, then handed one to me. I took it, my mouth waterin' from thirst.

"Tea," he said, moving his cup at an angle for me to see. "Good for you."

I pinched my eyebrows together. Anything Gram or Mama said was good for a soul generally tasted like furniture polish and smelled like rotten beets. The liquid was a light greenish-gold, and the scent was faintly minty, with a hint of something else I couldn't quite place.

Satan clucked his tongue. "It is fine. Good to taste." He took a long sip, and the sound of his slurping undid me.

Cautiously I touched the rim of the cup with my lips and tipped it ever so slightly. The tea was cool, and just the tiniest bit sweet. I drank deeper, then drained the cup. My eyes met Mr. Satan's as he poured me another. "It *is* good," I said. "What is it?"

"Sage and peppermint, with a touch of yarrow and honey."

I knew those herbs. Mama grew them all, just like Gram. "You make and prepare everything yourself? Even your medicines? What about special things? Stuff you can't make or grow?"

Satan inclined his head slightly. "I do buy Pixy Stix. Blue is my favorite."

*Pixy Stix?* I pictured Satan's tongue berry-blue.

There was a grin in Satan's eyes, if not on his face, and I couldn't help but laugh. I wondered if he'd shared that with Gloria. That would have won her over right then and there.

Thinking of Gloria made my chest ache. I knew I should be asking Satan about her, but I couldn't bring myself to do it. I didn't want Satan to think the only reason I was there was to pump him for information.

Which wasn't the full truth. I was also worried about what he might say. What his answers might be. *Did* he have something to do with Gloria's change, if not her death?

I took in a deep breath and tried to shift my train of thought. The air was drenched with springtime scents. Crocuses were just starting to bloom, their waxy white and yellow heads breaking through the dark soil along the cliff looking for all the world like sippy cups on sticks. We might have time to finish the wall before the rains started after all.

Satan put his empty cup back on top of the jug and reached for mine. I handed it over, my eyes trailing the jerky movements of his fingers. Every now and then it looked like he couldn't get them to do what he wanted. Instead of gripping a handle, his fingers would remain tight together or splayed like a Vulcan "live long and prosper" sign.

Either way, he didn't mention it, and I wasn't about to. I thought on how I felt every time Ray pointed out how small and skinny I was. Lousy. That's how. Like I'd never grow big enough to make him change his mouthy ways.

"You are frowning, Mr. Wilkins."

I looked up into Satan's blue eyes. "Just thinkin'."

"Something unpleasant?" Satan asked.

I flicked dirt clods off the cuff of my jeans. "My brother. He can be a real dog."

Satan was quiet, as if waiting for more.

"I mean, well, he has okay moments, but more times than not, he's just mean," I finished, surprised that I'd said it out loud. What would Mama think, me sharing thoughts of Ray with a stranger?

Satan nodded and took off his hat. "Families, sometimes, are like a great mystery. You live with them every day, but fail to unravel their true threads."

I scratched my head. I didn't know exactly what Satan meant, but even so, I felt like he got what I was sayin' about Ray.

Funny, but even in this short of a time, Mr. Satan didn't feel like a stranger anymore.


"Where you been, Gnat?"

Ray's voice at my back nearly made me jump clean out of my skin. I turned from cleaning up at the pump out front, wiped my wet hands on my shirt, then eyed my big brother.

He was lounging against the clothesline, his red hair combed all neat behind his ears. Being it was Saturday, I figured he must have been getting ready to go cruisin'.

"Out," I said, wondering if Ray was in a mood to start trouble.

He pursed his lips. "That so?"

"Yep."

"Out where?"

A chill stole up into the back of my legs. "Explorin'. Like always," I said, hoping to throw him off track.

Ray sniffed, then slunk off the pole. "You know, Gnat, you gotta get back on the horse once you get knocked down. Can't sit around bawlin' forever."

He stretched his arms above his head, joints popping, before his left hand came down on my shoulder— hard. I winced, the bruise still smarting after a week and a half.

"You need to go out and find yourself a new little girlfriend. This time one with less mouth and more going on in the eye-catchin' regions, if you know what I mean." He flashed his even white grin.

I knocked his hand away, my face burning. "Don't you say a word about Gloria."

Ray rolled his eyes. "See what I get for trying to be a good older brother?" He flicked my ear, and I yanked away. "Whatever, don't make no difference to me what you do. Chase tadpoles till you're blue in the face, Gnat, just don't come runnin' to me when it's time to grow up and there's no one around to help push you over the wall."

Hate blazed in my gut as he sauntered to Mama's Dodge. I couldn't believe she was letting him take her car. She'd have to drive his old clunker to the diner.

He left in a haze of rock dust, and my gaze fastened on the hill to the east. At least he didn't know about Satan.

Since we'd gotten the supplies, things had been moving faster than a chigger could find a warm body. Which was right fine, since after Ray's words, I'd felt a need for urgency.

Satan and I had managed to get the rest of the wood chopped and hauled, leaving us a respectable pile of timber. Tonight we cemented the uprights. Satan had guaranteed that we wouldn't see rain until Tuesday at the earliest. Plenty of time for the concrete to cure, according to him.

I didn't know what his source was, but so far he'd been dead-on right.

I chiseled off the last bit of oak to square off the end of a log, then moved on to the next. It felt good, chipping away at the wood until it held the best shape to be stacked against its neighbor.

Once we were done, Satan's house would stay perched on the hill another thirty years or more. Which I figured would make a lot of townspeople hoppin' mad.

"You have blessed hands, Mr. Wilkins."

Satan's voice startled me. I looked up. "Thanks." He was leaning on his shovel, his face flush with effort. He still called me Mr. Wilkins, even though I'd asked him to call me Billy.

"Your fingers know where the wood is willing to give way, and your heart knows how hard to tap or hammer to coax it to your wishes."

He sounded like Gram! I shrugged and went back to work. I wondered if Satan believed in knacks.

*Knacks . . .*

That tingling was back. Mama never put any stock in Gram's talk of knacks.

*Blame waste of time, talkin' about things that aren't true. Never were and never will be.*

I shuddered and looked over at Satan again. He was sitting on the ground, his arms cradling his head. "Are—are you all right?"

Satan smiled weakly. "Just a headache. Too much work, not enough to drink."

It was then that I realized Satan hadn't brought out the thermos. "I'll go get some. If that's okay?"

"Yes. That would be good." Satan rubbed the back of his neck. "The jug is on the table with the cups."

"Be right back." I patted Gertie and loped up the trail toward the cabin. I became slightly fuzzy-headed while closing the door tight behind me; I'd never been inside before.

My gaze automatically went to the shelves that lined the room. They were filled with books . . . and other things.

On tiptoe, my eyes were level with the shelf. Carvings. My eyes widened at each new creature: deer, bears, mice, birds. I forced my gaze to the kitchen table. Sure enough, the thermos sat there with two cups stacked on top. I knew I should take the tea and go right back down, but the carvings drew me like muddy water to new shoes.

My hand closed around a badger. Every aspect of it looked real, from the bristle of the hair on its neck to the fierce challenge in its eyes. Incredible. Some of the woods were dark, some honey-light, while others were the pale cream of a fresh sapling. I sat the badger back onto the shelf and wrapped my hand around a neat-looking bear. The wood was surprisingly warm, the texture rough in imitation of the animal's coarse hair.

As my eyes lifted, I almost gasped aloud. The bear had been hiding another figure.

This one wasn't an animal.

I put the bear down and picked the other carving up, blood pumping fast in my ears. It was a young woman sitting cross-legged on a stump. Her hair was tucked behind her ears, and I could even make out a sprinkle of freckles across her nose. It was Gloria, but not Gloria. The face was a little fuller, the smile softly sad, not Gloria's full, tenacious grin.

The door creaked.

I whirled, the figure clutched in my hand. Satan walked over and reached out. I set the carving on his palm. He took it gently, then placed it back on the shelf.

His gaze passed right through me as he went over to the table and sat. His hands trembled as he uncapped the thermos and poured two glasses. "Sit. Drink."

I did as he said, my heart beating so fast I felt sick.

We both took small sips. Our eyes never met, and no words passed between us.

# CHAPTER 16

"**C**ome on, Gnat! You gotta raise your glove to catch the ball!"

I gave Hog the evil eye and went back to scuffing my feet in the outfield. Hog was in shallow left, where most of the Kelseyville Mud Dogs grounded out. Other parishioners—men, boys, and some girls—were split into two teams and playing as if they were at the regional finals.

Don't know how I got roped into playing after church, but there I was. We'd attracted quite a crowd at Clemmens Park. Even Nick and his mama were in the stands. Few people sat near them, and Nick looked about as happy to be there as a feral cat boxed into a corner. I kept telling myself I needed to make an effort to spend time with him. He was Gloria's brother, after all.

"Knock it out of the ballpark, Dennis!" called Mrs. Williams from the stands.

Mr. Williams was up to bat. The muscles in his arms corded as he took a few practice swings. I balanced on the balls of my feet and tried to get my focus back on the game. There was a chance Mr. Williams *would* hit it out of the ballpark. Which would be fine. That would score them enough runs that our next turn at bat would be the end of the game, unless we matched their four-run lead.

One pitch, low and outside. The second one right down the pipe, but Mr. Williams didn't swing. Two more, one high, the other a nice slider that he swung at and missed. Two and two. Mr. Williams tapped the plate, showed his sweet spot, then held the bat at the ready.

I knew it was coming. Felt it even before the ball cracked along the inside of the bat. The ball soared, and Mr. Williams watched it for only a split second before dropping the bat and running for first.

Sure enough. That dang ball headed my way.

Luckily for me, clouds blurred the noonday sun, and I was able to track the ball as it arched over the infield. I kept my eye on it just like Ray taught me. To the left . . . more . . . more. My glove was up. Sweat trickled down the back of my neck.

*Keep it in sight. . . . Keep it—*

At the last second, it veered to the right, and my glove barely tipped the ball, knocking it sideways. It bounced onto the Kentucky bluegrass and rolled a few feet before stopping.

*Damn.*

I scooped it up and tossed it to Hog, who was hollerin' his fool head off. He caught it and pivoted smooth, rocketing the ball to home base, where Mr. Finnegan tagged out Preacher Cal.

"Third out! Wild Cats up!"

We filed into the dugout with everyone saying it was lucky Hog had an arm on him and that Preacher Cal ran about as fast as a trussed turkey.

Hog pounded me on the back. "Hey, nice try, Gnat. You almost had it."

"Yeah," I snorted. "A few more misses like that and you'll finally quit asking me to play."

Hog looked at me funny, his green eyes blinking.

I hadn't meant to sound ungrateful. I appreciated the fact that Hog tried to include me. Baseball just wasn't something I had a knack for, and I hated disappointing people. Especially Hog.

I sighed and leaned back against the concrete bench. When had things gotten so complicated? There was a time when even if I wasn't playing, sitting back and watching a game was a great way to kill a Sunday. Gloria and I would cheer for Hog, no matter what team he was on, and stuff our faces with Mrs. Keller's kosher dogs that she barbecued at each game.

It didn't take long for the game to end. Our first two batters struck out, and the third, Hog, hit a grounder and was thrown out. After all the congratulating and "good game, good game" talk, the onlookers and players began to head off to their cars or homes.

Seeing my chance, I jogged over to Nick, who was sitting at a picnic table waiting for his mama to come out of the restroom.

"Nick!"

He stopped chewing his cuticles and looked up.

I sat next to him. "Haven't seen you for a while. How are things going?"

He jerked his thumb at the restroom. "I've been stuck in the house with her, and there's, like, nothing to do around here."

I smiled. "Seems that way sometimes. But there're things, if you know where to look."

He picked at the splintered wood of the bench. "Oh, yeah? Looks to me like there's only fields and mountains and trees."

"Exactly," I said. "But there's lots of things in those fields and mountains besides trees. This time of year there's tadpoles in the streams. Salamanders, too. Lots of animals in the mountains. Deer, squirrels, birds. All sorts of stuff. Sometimes you can even find arrowheads, or pieces of quartz."

Nick frowned. "That doesn't sound very fun. Don't you guys have an arcade?"

I sighed. "There are a couple of machines at the pool hall downtown, but they don't take to kids hangin' out in there."

"This place is like some stupid movie where everyone's stuck in the '50s." Nick's eyes trailed people as they climbed into their station wagons and trucks.

It wasn't something I noticed much, but he was right. "Well, yeah. I guess. But that's not such a bad thing."

He snorted. "Are you going home now?"

"Yep."

Nick looked thoughtful. He swung his legs back and forth beneath the table. Part of me wanted to ask him to come along, show him some of those things I mentioned, but I had to help Mr. Satan this afternoon. The rains were close. I couldn't spend time goofing off.

Maybe Nick would be able to meet Satan eventually. I figured Gloria would like that.

Nick's mama left the restroom and headed our way.

Her shoulder-length wheat-colored hair, so much like Gloria's before all the black dye, waved out behind her in the breeze. She pushed it behind her ears and smiled as she walked up.

"Hello, Billy. It was good to see you playing today."

"Hello, Ms. Russell." I stood and ruffled Nick's hair, which earned me a fierce glare. "I've got to get going, but I'll come over one day this week, since school will be out for spring break. All right?"

I wasn't sure if Nick was going to answer. Finally he nodded. "That sounds okay."

It wasn't much, but it was a start. I said goodbye and hightailed it for Mama's Dodge.

Satan was sitting quietly on the porch bench when I went up after two o'clock. I cleared my throat and leaned on the railing. "We're ready to lay the final course of lumber, right?"

Satan nodded. "Yes. But not today. It is Sunday." He stood. "Come. Today we serve God by serving his creatures."

He smiled and led me to the work shed, where he handed me two buckets full of what looked like pine shavings, and a shovel. He took the same for himself, then led out Gertie and Gustav. Both goats had canvas bags strapped onto either side of their backs, crammed with what looked like young pines.

"Where are we going?" I asked as we headed into the forest, buckets banging against my hip.

Satan inclined his head north. " You will see."

We walked for nearly thirty minutes, the afternoon sun broken up by passing clouds. It didn't smell like rain, but it couldn't be far behind, and I wished we were working on the wall.

After climbing a redbud-choked hillside, we reached the top. I gasped. We gazed down at a secluded valley—that was completely bare of trees. Only ragged stumps remained of an area that must have been thick with pine and cedar. "What happened?" I asked.

Satan started down. "Clear-cut many years ago. There are a few pines that have regrown, but the soil is poor with no debris to strengthen and hold it."

As we walked, I noticed that there were new saplings at the edge of the glade. They looked about five or six years old, while the ones we'd brought out were probably about one or two. Further in, there were older trees, still not full-grown. "You've been planting here for a while," I stated, amazed.

"Myself, and my father and mother. Difficult to replenish what nature created over such a long time."

We stopped at a bare area near the outer ring of the glade. Weeds and underbrush had already been cleared, and the soil aerated. Now I knew what Satan did up on the mountain with his time. He wasn't just whittling and taking care of his home, he was taking care of the mountain, too.

"We plant here," he said, setting down his buckets and lifting the bags off of Gertie, then Gustav.

Satan showed me how deep and wide to dig the hole for the young pines, which we did, creating all the holes before placing them inside and backfilling with a mix of soil and wood shavings.

I tamped the soil around stem number six and stopped to gaze out over the clear-cut. "How many more areas are there like this? I've lived here my entire life and never seen one."

Satan took off his hat and wiped at the sweat on his brow. "There are more to the east. Not so many here, in this region."

There were several loggers who lived in Windell and even some in Kelseyville. In fact, logging and working for the paper mill were practically the only jobs that kept people here. "They don't do this now, you know," I said. "The clear-cutting. There's a company over in Windell that uses mules to clear. We learned about it in school."

Satan sat back on his heels and nodded. "Yes. It is less invasive. But on private land, loggers can take the trees how they see fit. It happens still."

The idea made my mouth sour.

Satan went back to digging. "Trees do need to be thinned in areas, though. Like where we are cutting for our wall."

Our wall.

Warmth seeped into my chest. I'd thought of it as Satan's wall, but the more we worked, the more I *did* feel as though a part of me was in those logs, too.

It took us about an hour and a half to plant all twenty of the young pines. As thick as the clouds were building, I didn't think we had to worry about watering them. I said as much to Satan and he agreed. "Do not worry, Mr. Wilkins. The rains will not be that heavy."

How could he be so certain? *And why is he always right?* I swallowed the fear away and kept on.

As we came upon the deer trail, Satan stopped, a queer look on his face.

"What is it?" I asked.

He didn't respond, just started off, and dread settled in my chest as I scrambled to keep up.

"Mr. Satan. What's wrong?"

Satan turned, nearly bumping into my face. I stepped back, my heart pounding.

"You should go now." His expression was tense, his eyes somber.

"Well, okay. I'll just put the buckets back."

He held out a hand. "Give them to me. You must go."

I did. I wanted to say something, but he didn't seem willing to listen. In fact, he seemed a million miles away.

"Uh, well, I guess I'll see you . . ."

"Billy James!"

I turned with a jerk.

*GRAM.*

She ambled out of the trees, her white hair blowing around her shoulders.

I ran over. "Gram! What are you doin' here?"

"I might ask you the same if I didn't already know." Her black eyes bored into me, but a flicker of worry tempered their usual fire.

She nodded to Mr. Satan. "Josef."

He half-bowed. "Mrs. Wilkins."

Her hand fell heavy on my shoulder. "We need to go, Billy. Come along." Her tone brooked no argument, not that I was up to giving one. My insides were jelly, my chest tight as a pickle drum.

I gazed at Satan, my body cold and hot all at the same time.

Satan nodded solemnly, buckets and shovels in hand. The goats stood beside him, staring at me with quiet eyes.

Had Satan known Gram was coming?

*How could he?*

I forced my gaze away and followed Gram down the hill. There were all kinds of questions I wanted to ask, but somehow I knew not to bother till we were out of earshot.

As we exited the trees at the bottom of the hill, there sat Gramp's old Ford. My jaw dropped. Gram *never* drove Gramp's truck. Not once in the entire twelve years of my life had I seen her behind the wheel. She started it up on occasion but never drove it anywhere. My eyes swiveled to her face.

"Close your jaw and get on in," she said, huffing around to the driver's side. "Took me long enough to get up this rutted deer trail they call a road. Time's a wastin'."

The passenger door opened with a rusty screech, and I climbed onto the plastic-draped bucket seat. Gram heaved herself behind the wheel and turned the engine over. It coughed twice, then revved to life, the cab rattling.

"Gram, what's going on?"

Without meeting my eyes, she threw the truck into gear and started down the hillside. "Your mama's on her way to Branson, to the Sisters of St. Augustine's Medical Center." She looked over with tired eyes. "Which is where we're headed, to see her."

# CHAPTER 17

ypass surgery. That's what the doctors kept saying. Triple bypass surgery. Plaque in the arteries. High blood pressure.

We'd gone in to see her after they'd run a bunch of tests. She was so yellowish-looking and puffy . . . and her eyes . . . flat. She didn't look like my mama at all. Gram pushed me into the chair by her bed and told Mama not to worry about anything at the house. Worry about getting better. Worry about gaining her strength back after the surgery, which was scheduled for early tomorrow.

Turns out Mama had gotten a flat in Ray's old piece-of-crap truck halfway to town. The stress of changing the tire combined with the sun had trigged a heart attack. It had been nearly an hour, they figured, before someone from town spotted her slumped in the front seat and drove her over to Dr. White's, who'd promptly pumped Mama full of blood thinners, got her stabilized, then shipped her off to Branson.

Doc White told Gram he'd warned Mama that this could happen and had advised her to go to Branson for tests over two months ago.

*Why didn't you go?* I wanted to ask Mama as I stared at her pale face and blue lips.

As we got up to leave, Mama grabbed my arm, her grip light as a feather. "Billy James," she whispered hoarsely.

I leaned in, the scent of ammonia and Lysol near gagging me. "Yes, Mama?"

"You . . . you take care of your brother, hear?"

My heart stopped. *Take care of Ray?* Ray should have been there to take care of you, I wanted to shout. Ray should have never had your car!

"Promise me, Billy James." Her grip tightened and her face tensed.

I looked at Gram. She nodded stiffly.

"Uh, okay," I muttered, hating the words and hating Ray more than I ever had in my entire life.

Her hand fell away and her face relaxed. In a matter of seconds she was snoring softly, and Gram pulled me into the hallway.

"You did fine, Billy. Just fine."

She rested a hand on my shoulder and I leaned in, every muscle in my body pinging with adrenaline.

Gram started down the hallway, pulling me along. "Don't you be worryin', Billy. They'll fix her up, and she'll be back to her old self in a matter of weeks, mark my words."

The drive back was as silent as the trip up.

As we came to stop, I spotted the truck out front.

Ray.

A picture of the night we came home from

Greystokes to find Ray and Company J on the porch filled my mind.

*That was before I decided Raymond Clay's made for better things than stacking boxes in some reject's warehouse.*

I remembered Mama rubbing her arm and chest when she had replied, *"You mean you up and quit, Raymond Clay?"*

Fury shattered everything inside me. I slipped out and made for the front door.

"Billy," Gram called from behind, her voice holding a note of warning.

I flung the screen door open and stepped inside, my head pounding. The floor was strewn with newspapers and empty soda cans. Clothes were slung over the couch, wadded in piles near the TV, and plates crusted with today's lunch littered the coffee table.

I found him slumped in Mama's good wingback chair, that damn book in his lap.

"Get out," I snapped.

Bloodshot blue eyes found me. "What?"

I knocked his leg off the arm of the chair. "You heard me. I said, GET OUT!" My temples throbbed, my face burned.

He staggered to his feet, his head cocked to one side, eyes narrowing. "Now I know you ain't talkin' to me, Gnat, 'less you want me to knock your head this side of Sunday."

"You broke Mama's heart, you piece of dog crap. *GET OUT!*"

His face darkened. So quick there was no chance of me jumping clear, his hand sent me spinning into the coffee table.

Red—then black, till my vision cleared and the pounding started again.

My fall busted that old coffee table in half, but I didn't care. *Stand up!* Ray was coming, eyes popping, hands reaching. . . .

I snatched up a piece of the table, bringing it to bear. I'd lay him open. *Crack his skull right in two.*

"Arggghhhh!" I swung.

Wood connected with flesh. I heard a grunt, then a curse. A hand fastened on my shoulder, yanking me backward.

"ENOUGH!"

I struggled, ripping my shoulder free only to come face-to-face with Gram. "Enough," she whispered.

The haze cleared, and reality fell on my head like a wrecking ball.

Purple. His face was purple, and he was holding his right hand against his chest. "You freakin' insect. You broke my hand!" he screeched.

I'd actually hit Ray.

Ray moaned. "How am I gonna pass my exam for the license with a broken hand?"

He stumbled backward and fell into Mama's chair. Another sob. "My hand . . ."

Every part of my body went cold, then numb. I felt sick.

*Take care of your brother, Billy James. . . . Promise me.*

I wrenched away from Gram, dropped the table leg, and shot for the door.

"Billy!"

Nothing would have stopped me. Not an army. Not

Gram. Not God. I could run like nobody's business. Running. That's what I was best at. Not fixing things. Fixing things was better left to people who gave a damn, instead of someone who didn't even know how to fix himself.

*I was broken.*

Just like Ray. Just like Mama's heart. Just like my daddy . . . broken.

# CHAPTER 18

ram stayed on at the house. Guess she figured one of us might rub the other out if she wasn't there to play referee. Us Wilkinses and our violent tendencies. Us and our hillbilly, homicidal ways.

She lectured me long and hard after getting back from the hospital with Ray. Part of me was beyond listening, which didn't sit well with Gram. "We got us some deep talkin' to do once your mama's home and well, boy." She finally "hmphed" before leaving me to my own devices.

There'd been no lecture about Satan, though. I didn't know why, but I was grateful. The only thing that could take my mind off Mama and Ray was thinking about the wall. And Satan. And how he could have possibly known Gram was coming up to get me.

I'd slept in the loft again. The hay was fresh, the night passably warm. It wasn't such a bad place to be. I'd pulled out Mr. Porter's letter and read it through ten—no, twenty times by the light of the half-moon. In the bright morning sunshine my eyes kept lighting on one line.

*I want you to know, Billy, that I'll be here if you need me.*

Did he mean it? Or was he trying to play nice? 'Cause I was thinking I might need him. That we all might need him. Mama, Raymond Clay, and me. Something was bad wrong with us. Mama laid up in the hospital, near to dying 'cause she didn't take care of herself. And Ray had been broken for as long as I can remember. Weird thing was, Ray hadn't said a nasty word to me since coming home from the ER with his cast. He sat sprawled out across the couch, quiet like I'd never seen Ray quiet. That had me powerful worried.

And then there was me. Me who wouldn't hurt "the eggs of a fly," as Gloria used to say, ready to kill. Wanting to hurt Ray so bad I could taste it—needed it like a dying man needs a preacher's words of redemption. Every time I thought on it my stomach soured.

Which was why I drafted a letter:

*Dear Mr. Porter,*

*I got your letter last week. I never knew much about my daddy, but I'd always suspected that his history was about as rocky as our hills.*

*I'm not writing for me, but rather for Mama. You can probably guess she didn't ask me to write. She doesn't even know I read your letter, but she's in a difficult spot right now, and I felt you ought to know.*

*She's due for surgery today on her heart up in Branson. We didn't know a thing about her having a problem till it landed her in the hospital. The doctors say she'll probably be all right once they give her some new arteries, but even after that, it'll take her time to recover, and then she'll have to make sure those new arteries don't back up with the junk that ruined them before.*

*I guess what I'm saying, Mr. Porter, is that I'd like to know if I could call on you if the need comes up? For Mama, of course, not for me. And, I wanted to ask, can you send my letters to a different address, on account of my not wanting Mama to be upset by them?*

I'd thought long and hard on this one. He could send the letters to Gram's postal box at the bottom of Cane Hill. Mr. Cathcart delivered to Gram's box once a week, and I was the one to bring her mail up to the cabin Saturday mornings. A perfect solution.

After scribbling in Gram's address, I signed my name and stuck the folded letter into an envelope I'd addressed.

Mama would just be going into surgery now, and Gram would be waiting on the outcome. She said there was no sense in me going with her this morning, as I wasn't allowed in the intensive care wing anyway. She'd given Ray his pain pills, and me strict instructions to stay out of Ray's way.

*Four whole hours of surgery.* The thought made me woozy, and I took off running, hoping to work everything out in a mad dash to the post office.

Which was a mistake. As soon as I showed my face in town, I was mobbed.

"—heard about your mama, Billy James."

"—are you boys alone up there?"

"—how long had she been sick?"

It was hard to field all the questions without seeming rude or impatient. I only wanted a stamp!

"One stamp, please," I said to Mrs. O'Dell at the counter.

"How's your mama, Billy?"

"She's in surgery right now. We'll know more later on."

"You boys need anything this week, you let us know, hear? We wouldn't want your mama to come back wonderin' why her boys weren't looked after proper."

A tingle passed across my shoulders at her words, friendly as they were. "Gram's with us," I said. "And we're old enough to see after ourselves for a time."

Mrs. O'Dell flicked a glance at my face. "Uh, hem. Well, we know how to look after our own."

With a shaking hand, I slapped on the stamp and dropped the letter into the slot, away from Mrs. O'Dell's curious eyes.

My feet seemed to have a mind of their own as they shuffled down the road toward Satan's hill.

"Billy James?"

Preacher Cal was on the road behind me in his blue Lincoln. I hadn't even heard him drive up. He leaned out the open window. "How are you, son?"

The preacher's gaze was dark with concern, but there was something else in that look.

"I—uh, I'm fine," I said, staring down at my feet, wondering if it was obvious what direction I was headed.

"I know your mama's having her surgery today. Figured you'd want to stay by the phone."

I raised my head. "Gram said we wouldn't hear for at least four hours, so I was trying to keep my mind off things."

His gaze went past me in the direction of Satan's

knob before coming back to rest on my face. "Son, you know you can come to me if you need to, right? No need to go beyond those that care for you for comfort or words of advice."

My stomach twisted, and I couldn't respond.

"Billy James?" His deep voice cut through my panic. Preacher Cal started to open his door. "Why don't you get on in? I'll take you to the house and sit with you till the call comes."

"No! I mean, uh, no thanks. I'm just gonna do some explorin' for a little while."

"I think it would be better if . . ."

My feet kept taking me backward toward the edge of the roadway. "I'll be fine. Thanks anyway!" I turned and melted into the woods before he could get his bulk out of the car.

I heard him shout my name, but I didn't stop. Didn't look back. With my heart knocking, I zigzagged at an angle to put me back on track to Satan's hill.

Satan was at the base of the knoll, working to leverage up the last course of crossbeams. My breath was coming fast, but I hurried over and grabbed one end, helping to set it in place. He looked over, his blue eyes steady.

"Mr. Wilkins, I didn't think to see you for some time."

"I didn't think you would, either. But, well, we have to get this wall done," I said in a rush, my face red, my mind still running through the scene with Preacher Cal.

He studied me for a moment before nodding. "Yes. Our time is less than it was. Mother Nature has revised her earlier proclamation."

I forced a smile. "Let's do it. We can finish today, I know we can."

Satan smiled his crooked smile. "Yes. I believe we can."

We set right to work. There were bolts to tighten. Crossbeams to put into place, and then braces to lay to ensure that the wall would hold no matter the load of mud working against it. We worked so quickly I hardly had time to worry about Mama, or Ray, or Preacher Cal.

Within two hours the last of the lag bolts and supports were in place. Satan and I stepped back.

I couldn't believe it. We'd done it. Built a retaining wall out of mostly natural material and the hard work of only two sets of hands.

"It looks good," I said quietly, remembering how each log felt under my hands. The grain of the wood, the sharp scent of pine, and even the thick residue of sap that had coated my palms.

"Yes," Satan said, hat in hand. He scrunched the brim as his gaze fixed on the seven-by-five-foot wall. "Yes, very good."

I looked at Satan from the corner of my eye. There was so much I wanted to tell him. About Mama. About Ray and Mr. Porter. Even about Nick. And then there was Gloria. Here we were done with the wall, and I hadn't asked him about Gloria.

Thunder cracked overhead and we both looked up. A fat drop of water exploded onto my forehead.

Talk about timing.

We started loading tools into the sledge. Within

minutes we were done, which was a good thing, as the heavens were settin' to split wide open.

"Heavy rains coming," Satan said almost to himself as we packed the last shovel and encouraged Penny up the path toward home.

After getting the animals settled, Satan and I retired to his front porch to watch the pour-down.

There was somethin' magical about a late spring drenching, especially watchin' it from a mountaintop porch. The entire woods go silent 'cept for the sound of water hitting trees, bushes, wood, and rock. *Thrum-a-dum-ping-thrum-dum-dum* . . .

I leaned back on Satan's bench and closed my eyes. Mama probably had another hour of surgery. I kept picturing how she'd looked in the hospital, and my gut got twisty with worry.

The bench creaked beside me. Satan was holding a small crate. He pulled out a chunk of wood and his knife, then set to whittlin'.

I forgot my hesitancy to sit too close as his fingers flew over the shapeless chunk of wood—cedar, this time—flicking off a shave here and there. He told me he didn't know what the final creation would be till he was practically halfway through. I'm not sure if I believed that. They all ended up being such fine replicas of their living models. How could he not know ahead of time?

Satan stopped and gazed at me thoughtfully. "Perhaps it is a good day to learn, yes?"

"You'll teach me?"

"I will give you the tools, and we will see if the

wood can teach you." He set his piece of cedar aside and held up the crate. "Choose," he said.

My eyebrows scrunched together as I rooted through the wood chunks. As I picked up one, then moved on to another, I realized that each piece had a particular "feeling." And it wasn't just their size and shape. Some were heavier, and some felt like they had more substance.

Fear buzzed through me. Our eyes met, and there was a sort of expectancy in his gaze. I gritted my teeth and plunged my hand back into the heap, pulling out the first piece my fingers closed on. I held it up as if I'd liberated a drowning pup and turned to Satan for his approval or look of disappointment.

I got neither. He was whittling, head down.

"Uh, okay, what now?"

His eyes rose, flicked to my shapeless lump, then to my face. "Now you ask the wood what it would like to spend the rest of its days as."

"You're kidding, right?"

He wasn't. He handed me a knife and showed me the different ways to safely hold the wood while shaving with the broad section of the blade, then how to use the tip for the finer work.

Satisfied that I had the basics, Satan nodded. "Before you make your first cut, you must ask."

"Do I wait for an answer?" I asked disbelievingly.

"I do not, but that is up to you." He bent back to his task and left me with knife in hand. I stared hard at that chunk of wood, trying to discern with my eyes what type of thing it should be. After five minutes, it still looked like a plain ol' knotty lump of pine.

*Ask.*

That's what he'd said to do. As if the wood had a mind of its own. What the heck. I squinted at the chunk and asked, *What would you like to be?*

No answer.

Not that I had been expecting one. I sighed and brought it closer to my chest. Placing the blade against the smoothest side, I sliced.

A thick scroll of wood fell to the porch. It was like cutting into a soft apple! I made more slices, rotating the wood. It was weird not knowing what I was doing. Not having a plan. After a time, I held out the chunk and frowned. It looked like Aunt Gessie May on a *good* day.

"This is silly," I muttered.

Satan reached out. "May I?"

I handed it over, careful not to let our fingers touch. I thought he was going to whittle away my mistakes, but no, he simply held it in his large hands and closed his eyes.

Prickles raced up my spine.

*What is he doing?* Praying? Communing with the spirit inside the wood?

After a minute, he opened his eyes. "When there are questions running through your head, it's hard to hear, yes?"

Mama's pale face swam to mind and I nodded. I hadn't realized I'd been thinking about her as I whittled, but he was right. I kept wondering why Mama ignored her doctor's advice. And why she let Ray get away with all he got away with. And why she never said anything about my daddy and didn't want me speaking with my grandfather.

A shiver galloped across my shoulders. "How do you stop thinking about—things?"

"How did it feel when you were shaping the logs? What did you feel in those moments?" Satan asked.

How *did* I feel? Whole. I'd felt whole in those moments. Complete. Like I knew everything I needed to know right then and didn't worry a bit about everything else.

"Yes," he said. I looked up to find him studying my face with those calm eyes. "Remember that feeling."

I jerked and looked at him sideways. *Could—did Satan just read my mind?*

He smiled softly and pointed to his eyes. "Your eyes, Billy. They communicate so well."

My mouth fell open. Before I knew what he was doing, he placed the wood in my hand and closed my fingers around it.

*He's touching me.*

His fingers were warm and dry. The tips, callused, scraped against the back of my hand as he withdrew. But there was no spark. No electrical current. No flashing lights or ringing bells. Just a touch, like any other.

I looked at the chunk of wood.

"Try to remember that feeling and start again."

That's when I realized he had called me by my first name. *He touched me and I'm fine.* I felt lighter. Relieved, somehow.

Time to get busy.

*Show me what to make you,* I said in my head, then started to whittle.

I made a small scrape. Then a larger one. The wood changed beneath my hands: bending, twisting even, as flakes drifted onto the battered oak at our feet.

A sense of "rightness" began to creep over me. That place that knew which wire to pull, or where on the trunk to shave, filled my body. It was a gentle whispering in the back of my head. A March breeze dancing through the pines.

After a time, I paused to actually *see* what it was I had been doing. A broad tail canted upward, a body, full yet sleek, and then the head . . . cocked to one side. I held the half-finished carving up. Thrown in stark relief, it showed its true color—black as the shadows at the forest's edge, dark as the sky on a moonless night.

*A raven.*

Now that I could see it clearly, my hands flew. I gave detail to its thick, sturdy tail feathers. Its proud chest, its sharp, nail-you-where-you-stand eyes, and partially open beak. I did the legs last, working carefully with the narrow end, chiseling them out and ending in tough claws.

Sweat stung my eyes. Hair and wood dust clung to my cheeks. I felt like I'd run a mile! But that didn't matter. I held the raven on my open palm, hardly believing what I'd done. It wasn't a great job. I'd nicked off a bit too much here and there. Not even close to what Satan could do, *but it was so right.*

I laughed, a wild sense of joy filling me. And the raven looked back as if to say, "It's about time!"

Satan stared at the bird with a mixture of sadness and affection flowing across his droopy face. "You have listened well. Raven is hard to hear and even harder to hold on to."

I didn't understand one word he'd spoken, but that

didn't matter. I'd done it. Something big. Something bigger than whittling a rough-looking bird. (Or pest, as most would call it.) I didn't even care a hang about analyzing the way I felt. It was enough just to feel it. To feel anything other than the grief, confusion, and fear I'd been buried under for the past few months.

Satan reached up and patted my shoulder. My body felt warm, and in that moment I knew why Gloria spent time with him.

*Crash!*

Our heads came up as one, and we stared through the rain to the dense pines beyond the path.

*More deer?*

The goats started bleating from the pen, their coarse voices making goose bumps erupt across my arms.

What I saw on Satan's face made my toes curl.

*Fear.*

Fast and true, it infected every part of his body. He dropped his hand from my shoulder and gripped the fox he'd been carving. He stood. My heart thudded.

"What is it?" I whispered, as if my voice might wake the dead.

Satan frowned. "You need to go. Quick, now. There's word of your mother."

I didn't question him. Didn't have to.

I handed him the raven and ran.

# CHAPTER 19

didn't stop till the stitch in my side flared to a burning stab.

*Mama.*

There was no sunshine. Clouds had filled the sky for as far as a body could see, and they were dark and low.

There were cars in the drive. Gram's pickup and two others. One of which was Preacher Cal's Lincoln. My insides froze, and my feet refused to move forward.

*Move, Billy . . . you can't stand in the yard all day.*

Somehow I found myself on the porch reaching for the screen door—and out came Ray. His eyes and nose were red, and he cradled his hand away from me as he stomped past.

"Where you been, Gnat? Think you can just leave all the worrying to big brother Ray? Is that it?"

"What's going on?" I asked Ray's retreating back.

He shrugged and wiped a hand across his nose. "Talk to Gram. She's inside."

My gut clenched.

*Mama.*

They were at the kitchen table. My eyes fixed on

Gram, then flicked to Preacher Cal and Sue Anne's mama.

Tired, puffy faces looked back, and my heart skipped a beat. "Gram?"

"Sit, Billy James. I've news of your mama."

My hands gripped the back of the oak chair. I couldn't sit—couldn't move. I tried to speak, but my mouth was as dry as a cattle pond in August.

Gram sighed. "Billy James, you look about ready to keel over. Sit!"

And I did. My body had a way of obeying even when my mind wasn't in the game.

"There were some complications today. Your mama's heart gave out during surgery—"

I leapt up. "What? What's that mean?"

A hot hand jerked me back into the chair. "Now you get ahold of yourself, boy, and let your grandmother finish."

"They finished the bypass," Gram said. "But she had to be put on a heart and lung machine to keep all her vitals in workin' order. Which means right now, she can't do what she needs to do on her own."

The leathery lines of Gram's face were as deep as the grooves in my raven's wings.

"She's not dead," I whispered.

Gram snorted. "You think your mama would give up that easy?"

I shook my head, my thoughts hazy. "What—what happens now? Do they need to do more surgery?"

"No. We wait for Sarah to start doing all the work on her own again. It might take some time, the doctors said. She had a big shock to her system, but they're hopeful."

*Hopeful.* Somehow that didn't sound right coming from Gram.

"We'll go see her tomorrow," I said, my fingers curled tight in my lap. "We'll help her get well."

"Now isn't that just the best attitude?" piped Mrs. Stoddard as she patted my arm.

Gram got up and grabbed a dish off the counter.

"Mrs. Stoddard brought you boys a chicken casserole."

She plopped it onto the table and fished a bowl out of the drainboard. A spoon followed, and within seconds steam floated into my face.

The lumpy white glob made my stomach roil.

"Your mama's the strongest God-fearin' woman I know, Billy," said Preacher Cal. "She'll be back in this kitchen fixin' you boys some of her fine home cookin' in no time."

As if that was all that mattered.

I stared at Gram and mouthed, *"Why are they here?"*

It wasn't as if Mama had died. We didn't need a preacher. Nor did we need free food like you'd bring to a wake. I opened my mouth to tell them that, when a knock sounded at the door.

"Hello? Mama?"

All eyes went to the screen. Sue Anne stood there, looking like a drowned rat.

"Baby!" Mrs. Stoddard jumped up and ran to the door. "I wondered where you had gotten to."

Sue Anne shuffled inside. Her fiery hair was plastered to her head, and her jumper was dragging with water and flecked with mud. What did she do? Jump in the river?

Gram walked down the hall. "I'll get some towels."

When Sue Anne noticed Preacher Cal, she gasped, hand to her mouth. "Oh, my. Did something . . . has something ha—"

"No." I stood, letting my spoon clang into the bowl. "Everything is fine. Right as rain."

Her blue eyes went wide. I stepped forward. She stepped back.

Mrs. Stoddard slipped in between us. "Billy's mama has suffered a setback, sugar plum, and he's a little upset."

"I'd like to go home, Mama," Sue Anne all but whimpered.

Mrs. Stoddard smoothed damp red hair off Sue Anne's forehead. "All right, baby. You do look peaked. And feel a bit hot." She took the towel Gram offered and wrapped it around Sue Anne's shoulders. "We'll take our leave now, Hester. You need anything, anything at all, you just holler."

Gram nodded once, then went back to putting dishes in the sink.

I squinted at Sue Anne. She *did* look flushed. Like she'd run a mile.

"I'd best be on my way as well, Hester." Preacher Cal pushed his bulk out of the chair and laid a hand on Gram's shoulder. "Oh, mighty Jesus, be with this family in their time of need," he rumbled, then walked over to me. He raised a hand to my head, and I backed up. The thought of him touching me gave me the willies.

I stepped away from his hand.

"You backing away from the Almighty, Billy?" Preacher Cal asked, all concerned and suspicious, as if I'd done something to indicate how messed up I was.

I thought of Mama and Ray, Gloria and Nick, and Satan. My stomach did a somersault, but I kept my place. "No, sir."

He smiled and slammed his paw onto my head, gripping it like an overripe melon. "Good Lord, be with young Billy James through this trying time. Keep his feet squarely on your glorious path to righteousness and protect him from the unrighteous influence of others."

Preacher Cal released my head and turned to Gram.

"I'll be back to check on everyone in the morning, Hester."

They all said goodnight, then tromped down our porch to their cars. I walked to the screen and watched as Sue Anne latched onto her mama's arm like a life raft. Then she tugged on Preacher Cal's shirt and whispered something in his ear. His eyebrows shot sky-high and his lips tightened.

He turned and stared at the house, and I shrunk back from the door, my insides curdling like cottage cheese. He said something to Mrs. Stoddard before getting in his own car.

Mud flew from the tires of the departing cars, and my head pounded in time with my heart, as if I'd done something bad wrong and was about to be called on it.

Gram and I went to sit with Mama the next day. She was still in a deep sleep from the meds, and she looked bad. "Talk to her," the doctors and nurses said. "Tell her anything and everything."

Well, "everything" wasn't an option, so I talked about the garden (which I had neglected to tend to the past four days), the deer I saw (but not whose hill I saw them on), and how everyone in town was concerned about her and wanted her to get well.

After a while, it was easier to do. I held her swollen hand and talked a bit about Nick and his mama. About what a shame it was that they'd been apart for so long. Then I found myself talking about Gloria. How much I missed her. How sad it was that no one in town understood her.

Things I *never* would have talked to Mama about were she awake. I don't know what came over me. Besides, I was supposed to be telling her about things that would make her want to *wake up*, not things that might make her want to *give up*.

Ray hadn't come to the hospital with us. He had gone on about how someone needed to stay behind to watch the house, as if we were expecting some roving band of outlaws to wipe us out. He kept saying it was what Mama would want him to do. Gram didn't raise a stink, just gave me a look that said "Leave it go, Billy."

And I did.

At least the doctors were certain that Mama's heart was doing better. The muscle was still tired and not pumping as regularly as it should, but she was breathing easier.

Back home I left Gram downstairs to give Ray the news, and went to my room. Checking to make certain

Ray or Gram weren't on their way upstairs, I then slipped into the hall and went into Mama's room, closing and locking the door behind me. My eyes scanned the area, and my heart shuddered.

I knew I shouldn't be in there. If she found out, she'd—

No. No she wouldn't, because she was in no condition to whup anyone. And she might never be again.

The thought left me cold and queasy as I pulled the light cord in Mama's closet. The scent of baked bread and lilacs wafted over me. Mama's clothes were crushed together on the narrow rod—shirts, jeans, slacks, and dresses. A few pairs of shoes sat at the bottom, and the top shelf was crowded with sweaters.

My hand shook on the door, and after a deep breath, I closed it and walked backward until I hit the bed, then sat.

An image of Gloria's box stashed under my bed popped into my head.

My fingers dug into Mama's mattress.

Maybe . . .

I got down on my knees and flipped her quilt up, exposing the underbelly of the frame. Pushing the stair stepper out of the way, I pulled out a package of vacuum-packed quilts. Behind that—boxes.

Shoeboxes. Plain and unappealing.

Ignoring the ache in my chest, I pulled one, two, three boxes out, then sat with my back against the bed. I placed one box on my lap. My fingers rested on the top, then I flipped off the lid.

Shoes. Dress shoes, to be exact.

Setting them aside, I gripped box number two, then lifted the cover.

*Jackpot.*

Pictures. Three-by-fives and smaller. I picked one up, my fingers shaky. Two ladies dressed in their Sunday best smiled back. It was Gram and Mama. I hardly recognized them. Gram's hair was dark, nearly black, but it was still in that bun. And Mama must have been about Ray's age, maybe a little younger. She was thinner, and her smile was wide. Her hair, a shade darker than my dusty brown, hung loose around her shoulders.

I turned it over. "Palm Sunday, 1978" was written in faded ink on the back.

There were more. Mama wearing shorts, twisting on a tire swing. I recognized Gram's giant oak. Mama and some girls in school dresses lined up in front of Kelseyville Middle School. Mama and Gramps playing checkers. Gramps was waving his hand at the camera, a scowl on his face.

There were so many. I kept digging. More school pictures. A particularly vivid one caught my eye. It was Mama and two other girls. They were all wearing cheerleader outfits, the bright red and gold of the Kelseyville Mud Dogs shocking against the white background of a wall.

Mama's hair was in pigtails, as was the other girls', which was why it took me a minute to recognize them. The one smiling on Mama's left was Mrs. Williams. Her blond hair sparkled. On the right was Ms. Russell. She was smiling, too, sorta.

I had no idea Mama, Ms. Russell, and Mrs. Williams had been friends in high school. I dropped it back into the "viewed" pile and took a deep breath. It felt like I was sneaking in someone's past.

And I guessed that's just what I *was* doing.

There were more pictures of the three of them. Some even older, when they were about my age. After 1978, there were no more pictures of Mama and Ms. Russell. There were some of Mrs. Williams. In fact, there were a few shots from her wedding, with Mama as one of the bridesmaids. I wondered when Mrs. Williams and Mama stopped hanging out together.

At the bottom of the box, there was a whole other layer of photos. I knew right away they were what I'd been hoping to find. My mouth went dry as I picked them up.

They were looped arm in arm, huge grins on their faces.

Mama and a red-haired man.

Daddy.

He looked a lot like Ray. Or rather, Ray looked a lot like him. But he was bigger, his arms thick with muscle, which was clear to see in his sleeveless T-shirt.

Maybe my arms would grow after all.

I ran a finger across Daddy's face and tried to see myself there. Maybe a little in the eyes, wide and open. I shuffled through other pictures. Daddy and Mama at church. A wedding picture. Mama looking happy as a clam, and Daddy looking, well, resigned. Daddy holding up a stringer of catfish. Then a clutch of doves. Daddy and Mr. Williams leaning against an old dogwood that had been split by lightning.

Then little Ray came along. There were pictures of

Mama with baby Ray. Ray was just as red and pimply as an infant. Ray in diapers hamming it up for the camera. Ray in the tub, his shock of red hair standing on end.

My hand shook as I gazed at a picture of Ray and Daddy. Daddy was holding baby Ray up, a big, even white grin on his face. The next one, Ray and Daddy were standing in front of Gram's cabin. Following that, Daddy swinging Ray around by his arms, Ray laughing.

There were more.

The next few were when Ray was about five or six. His small arms were wrapped tight around Daddy's neck. Daddy had a cigarette hanging from his lip, and his gaze jagged to the left.

Something inside me lurched, leaving me dizzy.

The last two were similar. Ray holding on to some part of Daddy, his leg, hand, shirt, and Daddy not smiling. Not looking at anything, really, that I could tell.

I leaned back, closing my eyes, recalling every single piece of Daddy that I could from the pictures. His red, mussy hair, his wide blue eyes. His strong arms and chest and freckles.

I rubbed a hand across my face and sighed. Finding the pictures hadn't done anything to ease my mind. In fact, now there were even more questions burning one on top of the other.

Mindful of Ray downstairs, I quietly piled the pictures back into the box. I slipped the one of Daddy and Mama into my pocket.

Downstairs the kitchen was dim, and it looked like Gram had already left.

As I started for the refrigerator, my foot knocked into something smack in the middle of Mama's braided rug. Ray's book.

I squinted and read the cover: "How to Be a Bounty Hunter in 10 Easy Steps." Well, 'course, if it wasn't easy, Ray wouldn't have given it a second thought. As I tossed it onto the chair, pages floated loose to the floor.

*Had I torn the book?*

My heart skipped a beat, but when I picked the pages up, I realized they were lined and folded notebook sheets.

I scanned the papers, tongue pressed against the inside of my cheek. They were study notes:

1. *Never assume you know a situation before you arrive, but always find out as much as you can about your target before committing to an action.*
2. *Knowledge is everything. Bounty hunting is 10% contact/apprehension and 90% investigation in prep for apprehension.*
3. *If you carry a gun, you'd better be prepared to use it.*

If I hadn't recognized Ray's handwriting, sloppy as it was, I would've thought the notes were someone else's. An image of Ray sitting by the lamp and spending hours taking those notes before I wrecked his chances filled my head.

Guilt, fresh and sharp, hit me.

I sat the book on the table and walked into the living room. Ray was slumped on the couch, eyes closed, but his good hand was squeezing a handball.

"Uh—Ray?"

No response.

"Ray?"

He cracked open one bleary eye. "What?"

"Uh, well, uh . . ."

Two eyes this time. "Godsakes, Gnat, what do you want?"

I almost turned and left. But I couldn't. I had to ask him. "Do you think Mama's going to be okay?"

Ray's gaze left my face and fastened on the rain-slick window pane. "Sure. She's tough."

"But what if she's not? What'll we do then?" I whispered.

He finally sat up. "What do you want me to say, Gnat? That everything will be perfect? That Mama will come back good as new and you'll get to go back to wandering all over creation without a worry in your head? Is that what you want to hear?"

"Uh, I—I was just wonderin' what we were gonna do if Mama can't work for a while. How are we gonna help her out?"

"Who do you think's been helping out already?" He swung his legs around to where he was facing me and pointed to his chest. "Me, that's who. I've been paying the gas bill for over year. Bet you didn't know that, did you, genius boy?"

"Why were you doin' that?"

He barked laughter, then crossed his arms. "You're so smart, you tell me."

"We—is Mama broke?" I asked, my voice cracking.

Ray gestured wildly. "Have you looked around recently, Gnat? You think you live in a palace?"

Our house wasn't fancy, but it was okay. Mama took care of things the best she could. "Mama works all the time and she never said anything about not being able to pay the bills."

He stood and I backed up. "Sure, she works all the time, but how much do you think she gets paid? Daddy might have gotten the loan on this house, but he left Mama with the mortgage and all the bills to pay. What she makes at the diner barely covers the house, phone, and food bills. Then there's the animals to feed." His eyes narrowed in on me. "And school stuff for you, lunches, books, crap like that."

Fingers of dread yanked on my insides. "I . . . uh, how much does all that cost?"

A snort. "Enough. 'Course you wouldn't know anything about that." Ray leaned down, his face full of pretend sympathy. "You're the favorite. The golden boy who can do no wrong. Mama wouldn't want to worry you, might distract you from all the great things you're gonna do."

His words left me queasy. I pushed Ray away and moved to the doorway.

"That's right, Gnat. Run away and hide. You're good at that."

Heart thudding, I turned. "You wanted to take the test in Windell," I said, understanding a piece of Ray for maybe the first time ever, "to help out *Mama*?"

"Don't matter now." Ray shrugged. "The test is next week and there's no way I can take it. I'll have to beg old man Deacon for my job back. I can't go another month without work."

Ray, beg? I couldn't picture that, but he'd find some way to make it happen. I looked at Ray's cast. "I—I'm sorry about your hand."

It was the first time I'd said it, even though I'd thought it lots of times. Ray didn't say anything back, and I figured that was okay. For all the times Ray'd whupped on me, he'd never broken anything. Split my lip, yeah, but no broken bones.

As I turned to leave, Ray's voice trailed me: "Mama will be okay, Gnat."

The rain was a steady drizzle that chilled my bones and soaked my feet on my way to the Stop 'n' Shop downtown. I was so full of worry, I imagined I'd drown in it long before the rain could wash me away.

I was halfway down the cereal aisle before I noticed the stares.

The back of my neck prickled, and I looked up. Mrs. Dewitt was there with her two tots. She looked away and shooed the kids to one side of the aisle. At the meat counter, other eyes trailed me, but everyone kept a distance. There were no concerned greetings. No questions about Mama. Not a bit like it had been the other day.

I rang the service bell and waited for Beavis's daddy, Mr. Waldorf. He ambled out from the back, stopping short of the counter when he saw me.

"Billy."

"Hi, Mr. Waldorf. I'd like one of those corn dogs, please."

He seemed to be considering something, his eyes pinned on my chest. "How's your mama?"

A normal enough question. But something in the way he said it left me cold. "She—she's not awake yet. But they're hopeful." There was that word again—*hopeful.*

He sighed. "That's good, then. Sooner she comes home to you boys the better."

I waited for him to get my food. But he just stood there.

"I heard your brother broke his hand. Can't take that test in Windell now."

My breath caught in my throat. "Uh, guess not."

"Your family's sure had a rash of bad luck as of late."

"I—guess." Sweat mixed with rain dripped off my forehead and splattered onto the linoleum floor.

"Strange. All that stuff happening in such a short time."

Despite my hunger, I knew I couldn't eat a thing. "Forget that corn dog. Thanks anyway." I rushed through the double doors, trying to wipe Mr. Waldorf's worrisome face from my mind.

*What's wrong with me?*

Thinking back to how peculiar everyone was acting, I thought, *What's wrong with them?*

"Billy James."

Blinking water out of my eyes, I turned to face— Preacher Cal.

"I'd like to talk to you for a moment."

He grabbed my arm and hustled me down the street toward the chapel. Stares followed us the entire way, as if we were part of some peculiar rainy-day parade.

We went inside the chapel, the dim interior swallowing us up like a cave. Preacher Cal led me over to a pew and sat. Being as he was holding my arm, I had no choice but to sit as well.

The preacher's heavy aftershave filled my nostrils and my stomach lurched.

"Son, I was told that you've been spending time with Josef Satan. That true?"

I gripped the pew.

*Sue Anne*. That day at the house. The crash we'd heard at the cabin. Her wet, flushed face. *She'd been spying on us.*

Anger burned through me, from the bottoms of my feet all the way to the top of my head.

"Billy James?"

Preacher Cal's penetrating dark eyes were somber and unblinking. I stood. "I don't have to answer that," I said, my voice cracking.

The preacher's hand jerked me back into the pew. "I'm afraid you do." His expression had gone hard like it did when he was gearin' up to shout the devil down in a Sunday sermon. "*Have* you?"

"Yes!" I hollered right into his face. "I have, okay?"

So quick I didn't have time to move, Preacher Cal gripped my head. "Oh, Lord, please protect this boy from the wickedness of those who do not follow your creed and would lead our youth astray."

My ears buzzed as he continued to boom. "Cleanse this young servant of—"

I began to struggle. "Stop!"

Preacher Cal released my head but kept a firm grip on my shoulder. "Son, you don't understand." His eyes looked feverish. "Gloria spent time with that devil before she passed, befriending him out of pure spite for this community and her mother's wishes."

I stopped struggling.

*They knew.*

They'd known all along.

I couldn't breathe. Everything was wrong—upside down.

The preacher leaned in, his warm breath brushing my face like a furnace blast. "She was warned not to. You think we said what we did all these years just to hear ourselves say it?" He shook me slightly. "We all figured after Gloria's untimely passing, you'd have enough sense to stay away, but by God somehow he got to you."

Preacher Cal's eyes snapped with fury as his fingers tightened on my shoulder. "And your poor mama and brother, bearing the brunt of your foolish choices."

"That's not true," I whispered, the room spinning.

"It's God's own truth, boy, and the sooner you see that the better. We're gonna get this resolved before your mama comes home. And as God is my witness, it's not ever going to happen again."

I yanked free and scrabbled out of the pew and into the aisle.

He stood, his bulk filling the space between us. "Son, sit yourself back down."

"No, sir," I whispered before turning and sprinting toward the door. My hands hit it with such force, they struck the clapboards with a *thwack!*

And I was outside.

Running.

Eyes followed me. I could feel them burrowing into my back. From the Sunshine Grocery. The corner gas station. Then Mr. Williams's hardware. He was out front loading up someone's truck.

"Billy!"

I didn't stop. Couldn't stop. Water stung my eyes, and mud flew up onto my jeans and jacket as my feet squelched into the roadway.

At that moment, I knew I'd never stop running in Kelseyville.

# CHAPTER 20

stood at the foot of Gloria's final resting place, hands limp at my sides, water dripping off my hair and rolling down my jacket sleeves. She didn't have a headstone yet. There was just a little metallic-looking marker shoved into the ground and a small urn of wet fake roses.

They should've been daisies. Daisies were Gloria's favorite, on account of all the different colors they came in. Daisies were simple, she used to say, but pleasant, with no perfumey smell to muck up their looks.

I sat, hard, water squishing beneath my butt and seeping into my jeans, but I didn't care. My breath still came in ragged gasps, and my throat was raw as August apples.

"They knew, Gloria. They knew that you were seeing him." My gaze fastened on the rim of mud around the grave. "They think he's responsible for what happened to you. And for Mama, and even for me breakin' Ray's hand." I choked out a laugh. "Wasn't Satan did that. Well, maybe it was the *real* Satan working inside me. But it wasn't *our* Satan."

I pulled my knees up to my chest and fought the

tears that threatened. There was no doubt in my mind that Preacher Cal believed Kelseyville's Satan was pure evil, like I believed the sun would rise each day and the moon each night.

Wrong as that was, there had to be a reason. Something . . .

*It's time.*

I blinked tears and rain out of my eyes and stared hard at Gloria's grave.

*It's time, Billy. . . .*

"I know it," I whispered, standing and heading for home.


I took Gloria's box up to the loft.

My fingers burned as I pressed the clasp, easing it over the teeth of the latch. It popped off with a sigh, the box creaking like a long-buried coffin. Even though I was wet and shivering like it was the dead of winter, sweat beaded on my forehead and rolled down my neck.

*Like the day Gloria gave me the box.*

With a shaking hand, I pushed the lid open. The box was jammed full. My fingers brushed the top items. Letters. Piles of them. I grabbed one, turned it over, and read the name on the outside:

*Nicholas Dugan*
*1036 Capistrano Ct.*
*Palm Springs, CA 92262*

Of course. Her brother. There was another, and another . . . all addressed to Nick. The letters were sealed, and I didn't think it right to open them. They even had stamps in the right-hand corners.

Why hadn't she mailed them?

I set them aside and went back to the box. That's when I spotted the letter jammed up into the lid. I wrenched it free. It wasn't addressed to Nick.

*Billy*—it read. No address. No stamp.

With shaking fingers, I opened the flap and pulled out several sheets of cream-colored paper. Her tiny, slanted writing filled each page. And it was as if she were sitting across from me, legs folded, hands reaching impatiently for the letter.

> *It's about time you got around to this. I figured it might take a hundred years, but I knew eventually you would.*
>
> *Here's the hap. If you're reading this, I'm either six feet under or so vegetized that I might as well be.*

There was a space in the letter at this point, and a small slash, as if she'd accidentally jerked the pen across the page.

> *Guess I'd better start at the beginning. You'll likely be shocked, but I can't help that. Besides, you're used to me shocking you, right?*
>
> *First, I've been feeling weird since late January, before I met up with Satan, just so you'll have it straight in your head. I get these headaches, and my stomach's been upset, too. They started out like regular headaches, but the last couple of days they've felt like someone driving nails into my head. I didn't tell Mama. She has enough to worry about, and you know my mama doesn't handle "situations" very well. I didn't tell you, 'cause you're likely to tell your mama,*

*then she'd tell mine. You know how it works. Anyway, that's all changed. Mama's taking me to the hospital tonight. We're leaving in about five minutes, which is when I'll run this box over to your house.*

*I guess you're wondering what this has to do with the way I've been acting. Well, nothing, really, or maybe it does. Either way, I realized in February how ticked off I was at this town and everyone in it. Even you, Billy. I don't say this to hurt you, but you're a lot like everybody else here when it comes to not wanting to rock the boat, you know?*

*That one day when Satan came into town in mid-February, it hit me: I was just like everyone else, keeping secrets, and for what? So I wouldn't stand out? So I'd fit in?*

*What a joke! I never fit in here, Billy. I tried, maybe not real hard, but I did try for my mother's sake. Seeing Satan walking down the alleyway that day, I wanted, NEEDED, to show everyone how UNlike them I was. And I was going to do that by touching Satan.*

*When I grabbed him, nothing happened. He didn't gobble me up—I didn't fall over dead. Nothing. Which, of course, got me to thinking about why the whole town would lie to keep us away from some poor, ordinary guy.*

I flipped the paper over, my eyes zooming back to Gloria's words.

*So I decided to spend time with Satan. I went to his cabin. Pestered him until he realized I wasn't going to go away. It took him a while to open up, but he did. I learned about his family. They're from the Czech*

*Republic. Did you know that? He was born there, and went back to live there when he was older. I tried to get him to talk about growing up in Kelseyville, but he was tight-lipped about that. He did talk a lot about his parents, though. How his mama was really skilled with herbs, and how things had been bad in his home country, which is why his parents had settled here.*

*He's an intelligent guy, Billy. And what he can do with wood! He reminds me of you, in a lot of ways. He's good with his hands and watchful about nature and people. And the best part is, he doesn't judge me. Doesn't comment on my hair, or my clothes, or even my attitude, which is, I'll admit, rough sometimes.*

*But the more time I spend with him, the more I realize that there IS something different about him. Something strange, and maybe even powerful.*

I had to stop for a moment. Hearing Gloria's voice so clearly in her written word was overwhelming. After a few seconds, I smoothed a trembling hand over the next crisp page and read on.

*There were clues. Like sometimes he'd answer a question BEFORE I asked it. I think he has some sort of ability to . . . know things before they happen? Or maybe tell the future? I'm not sure what to call it, but he definitely has some type of knack that we don't.*

*Plus, he DID avoid touching me. I thought that was especially weird, since the first time I'd grabbed him, nothing had happened.*

*Well, today while I was with Satan, I was having one of my bad spells. My head hurt, my stomach was upset, and right then and there, I decided to make Satan touch* me. I thought maybe it would be different if he touched me, instead of me grabbing him. While we were hoeing out scrub, I faked a fall, and he caught me.

Billy, you should have seen his face. I swear it went scary-white. He always looks sort of sad, what with his face kinda droopy the way it is, but right then he looked downright horrified. He set me on my feet and insisted I go see a doctor right away.

Well, you know me, no way I was gonna do what he said without knowing why he thought that. It was brought on by the touch, I was sure. I'd been waiting weeks for him to admit he had some special knack. So I refused to see a doctor till he answered all my questions.

Which would have worked out fine if I hadn't collapsed right then for real. Guess I must have looked really bad, all crumpled up on the ground like I was, because the next thing I saw was Satan's white face looming over me. He scooped me up and started down the hill without another word.

Before I knew it, there we were on my doorstep, with Satan ringing the bell. I'll never forget Mama's face when she opened that door. I didn't think anyone's face could get whiter than Satan's, but hers was. He handed me over and told my mama to take me to the ER right away.

Mama didn't say a word. She just nodded and closed the door, her face frozen in this weird expression. After a minute she laid me on the couch and went straight to the phone to call someone to take us into Windell. I told her I was fine, but she wouldn't listen. We have to wait about fifteen minutes for Mrs. Denham to get over here with her Chevy, 'cause you know our old clunker would never make it.

*I don't know what's going to happen after that. We'll see. I suppose I'd better get down to the nitty-gritty.*

*I need you to help me, Billy.*

*First, I DEMAND that you NOT feel guilty or otherwise freaked out that you didn't help me before whatever happens happened. I know you, Billy— you're a guilt expert. Forget it. It was my choice to freeze you out, and we both know how good I am at getting what I want.*

*Second, I need you to mail the letters as soon as you open the box. They're to my little brother in California. Sorry. Another big shock. I wanted to tell you about him plenty of times but couldn't bring myself to do it. It was like, how would I explain why I hadn't told you before?*

*Maybe because you'd want to know why he never came to visit, or why my mama left him behind, and I don't have good reasons for that. All I know is that my daddy in California didn't give a rip about us, but he loved Nick.*

*Third, I want you to talk to Satan. He'll probably blame himself for whatever happens to me, and that's ridiculous. I know you're afraid of him, Billy, but I wrote all I wrote so you'd be able to see how wrong we all are about him. So you wouldn't be afraid. Or, even if you ARE, that you'll know enough to somehow get past it. I know you can do it. And I know you'll love Satan once you get to know him. Make sure he realizes how important the time I spent with him was. I wish I could tell you exactly why the town hates him. I bet your Gram would know. If anyone can get her to spill the beans, it's you, Billy.*

*And last, but not least, I want you to dig down into the very bottom of the box. Go on! Do it, then come back to the letter.*

Shoving aside trinkets and scraps of paper, I burrowed to the bottom.

It was lying on its side. For a minute I thought that I was seeing things. I plucked the carving out of the box and stared at it in awe. There was finer detail in Gloria's raven. Richer detail. But the pose was almost exactly like the bird I did at Satan's. Even down to the canted head and sharp, intelligent eyes. My chest felt so tight it was all I could do to draw a breath.

I set the bird beside me and went back to the letter, my head spinning.

> *Pretty cool, huh? Satan carved that for me. He tried to teach me to whittle, but I'm an accident waiting to happen. He told me he wanted me to have it. He said that of all the spirits he frees from the wood, Raven comes along only once in a great while. He said the raven is a messenger of important change.*
>
> *That wooden bird you're holding makes sense to me, Billy. I can't explain it, but it feels like part of me IS the raven, you know? Everyone thinks the raven is a pest. It's forever where it's not wanted, bold, demanding, and despite all that, beautiful in its own way, don't you think? There is a sense of power in the raven. Something magical.*
>
> *I don't know. Maybe that's all wishful thinking. Maybe I want so bad to be beautiful, strong, and powerful, I'm making all this up just so I'll feel better.*

"NO!" My shout echoed off the beamed ceiling, sending a family of barn swallows flitting out the loft door. "It wasn't wishful thinking, Gloria. You were everything you said and more."

And I knew without a doubt that the raven I'd carved up on Satan's hill had somehow been a message from Gloria. Some little part of Gloria telling me that big change was coming.

*Mama. Ray. Mr. Porter. Satan. Nick.* Change that would stick with me no matter what. No matter if I tried to ignore it. Hid from it. Buried it. The raven knew change was coming. And Gloria knew, too.

> *I've got to stop. Mama's breathing down my neck.*
>
> *I want you to hold on to my raven, Billy. I hope the message of change it brings you is a good one. One that can make a difference.*
>
> *Don't forget to mail those letters to Nick. I've been the worst sister in the world, and I hope the letters can at least convince him that I care. I do. I think of him every day. And so does Mama.*
>
> *You are the best friend a body could ever wish for, Billy. I guess life is all about learning how NOT to let fear make all the decisions for you. I know you'll do a better job of it than me. You were the brighter and braver of us, even though you'd probably never think so. Ask the raven. He'll tell you it's true.*
>
> *Gloria*

The pages drifted to the floor, the afternoon breeze teasing the corners as they fluttered against the dusty wood. It was several minutes before I could think clearly. I didn't cry. I was finally out of tears.

# CHAPTER 21

It had taken me a good long bath and several glasses of Gram's cocoa to heat up and dry out after my visit to Gloria's resting place last night. It was morning now, and the house was empty. Ray'd gone to Windell to see about getting his job back, and Gram was taking a spell with Mama. With all the quiet, my head was near to bursting with Gloria's letter and Satan's knack.

And then there was Nick.

I took the picture of Mama and Daddy out of my back pocket and stared hard. Did Nick miss his daddy? Did he miss Gloria?

*Hard to miss someone you never knew.*

I tucked the picture away and took the shortest route to Gloria's house. The small, gingerbread-style home sat dull and quiet in the gray overcast. I trudged up the walkway, my gaze resting on everything so painfully familiar. The peeling paint. The ripped screen door where Gloria's cat, Merlin, came and went at will. The porch swing that Gloria and I used to sit on in the evenings watching the sun sink behind Duard's Peak.

After a deep breath, I knocked. Within seconds Ms. Russell opened the door.

"Billy James? This is a surprise." She stepped back and opened the screen. "Come on in. Nick's watching TV."

We walked into the living room, where Nick sat glued in front of the TV.

Ms. Russell walked over and turned off the set. "Someone's here to see you, Nick," she said before disappearing into the back of the house.

I crouched in front of him. "Hey, Nick."

His eyes rose slowly, his mouth a hard, thin line. "I didn't think you'd come."

My thoughts drifted back to Gloria's letters. "I always keep my promises."

He fiddled with his jean cuffs and avoided my eyes. "So, what do you want?"

"It's not me that wants something, it's your sister."

That got his attention. He looked up. "Are you trying to pull some psycho mumbo jumbo on me?"

I shook my head. "Nope. No foolin'. Come on. There's something important I need to show you."

Mistrust was stamped across his face, but he got up and followed me to the door all the same. On the way out, my gaze strayed to a picture on the wall. One I'd probably walked by a hundred times before yet never noticed. I stepped closer, my breath stuck in my throat. It was a girl sitting on an old stump. With longer hair and a few more years, it could have been Gloria.

"What are you looking at?"

Nick's voice brought my head around. "This picture. Did you know Gloria looked a lot like your mama?"

He scooted over and peered at the photo. "Oh, yeah?"

"Yeah," I said, staring right along with Nick. I stepped closer, my nose nearly touching the dusty glass.

"Let me see," grouched Nick, pushing me aside. "That's my mom?"

"I think so," I mumbled. My mind filled with images of Satan's cabin and his carvings. I swallowed and pushed the screen door open. "Let's go."

The barn was cool as we went inside, and as we climbed into the loft, Nick grunted a little less with each pull up the worn ladder.

"Have a seat," I said quietly once we'd made it to the top.

He crossed his arms. "What are we doing in this stinky barn?"

Ignoring his attitude, I retrieved the box and sat, facing him. "To talk about your sister. This box is Gloria's."

His sneer fell into a breathy "Oh." Then he sat and crossed his arms again, his lower lip thrust out. "Prove it."

I opened the box, then turned it so he could see inside. "She gave it to me not long before she passed, but I didn't open it till recently."

His eyes fastened on the contents of the box. "Why?"

"Why what?"

"Why did you wait so long to open it?"

"Because I was afraid of what I might find inside," I said softly.

Nick looked at me, his expression tense. "My mom

wouldn't have opened it either. She's afraid of even thinking about Gloria. Is—is it really hers?"

I held up the pile of letters. "Yes. Everything in here is, was, hers."

He leaned in. "What are all those?"

"Letters she wrote to you, Nick."

His gaze narrowed. "I don't believe you."

"It's true." I opened the first letter and pulled out two purple-lined pages. "This is her handwriting, and it's addressed to you. Do you want to read them?" I asked quietly. "Or maybe you'd rather have your mama read them to you?"

"No way!" He grabbed the pages and squirmed back. "I can read. I'm almost eight, you know."

I nodded and stood. "I'll head on down to the workshop. I've got some toasters to work on. If you need anything, just holler."

"Wait!" He looked lost sitting there, his eyes full of doubt. "You—you can stay if you want. I might have a question or something."

I sat back down. "Okay. I'll read my comics while you read your letters. After that we can talk if you want."

He nodded, his gaze zeroing back in on Gloria's words.

As the minutes ticked by, I snuck glances. Nick was mouthing the words as he read, emotions rolling across his face. Confusion, delight, consternation.

He looked up. "Billy? What's s-sur . . . uh, S-U-R-R-E-A-L mean?

Before long I was reading the letters to him start to

finish. Turns out he *was* a good reader, but Gloria's vocabulary left us both scratching our heads. Lucky for us, she wrote definitions in parentheses next to the bigger words.

Gloria's letters to Nick were sort of how you'd write in a diary. She told him all about her daily life. Friends, fights with their mama, and even some of her fears. Most of the stuff I knew about, but there were some things she hadn't even shared with me. I said as much to Nick and watched him puff up with pride.

"Bet she knew *I'd* understand," he said, pointing to his chest, and I agreed.

They were so alike in certain ways—even though they'd lived apart most of their lives. Tough. That's how I'd describe Nick and Gloria. Tough and unwilling to roll over and take whatever life handed them.

We decided that three letters in one day were plenty. Gloria's words and ideas were floating around in Nick's head like a truckload of fresh fertilizer. Packed with good things and energy to spare, but needing time to mellow. We agreed to meet in the loft every day after supper until all the letters were read.

Nick carefully folded the letters and put them back in their envelopes. Gloria's letters, his mama, and I were the only link Nick had, or would ever have, to his sister.

I reached into the bottom of the box and pulled out Gloria's raven. "Here," I said, handing it to Nick as we stood by the ladder. "This is for you, too. She wanted you to have it."

Which wasn't the whole truth, but it felt right.

Nick took the bird, his brow crinkling. "What the heck is it?"

"A raven. It was carved by a friend of your sister's."

He turned it over, just like I did the first time I saw one of Satan's carvings. "Wow. It looks so real."

"Yeah. Everything this guy carves looks that way," I said, thinking of Satan's cabin, and the girl on the stump, her hair pushed behind her ears. We put the box away and climbed down the ladder.

I walked Nick home with his mouth workin' a mile a minute about a sister he was just beginning to know, and Satan's raven clutched in his hand.

# CHAPTER 22

'd dropped Nick off at home, with a solemn oath to take him back to the loft to read more of Gloria's letters tomorrow after supper, then walked up to Gram's cabin.

She was on the porch. I sat beside her on the swing and stared at my hands. "How's Mama?"

"Better. Still asleep, though. Don't mean nothin' bad. Doctors said it was normal for a body to go into a deep sleep to help regain its strength."

Seemed like we were all trying to convince ourselves that Mama was fine. But she wasn't. None of us were.

*If anyone can get your Gram to spill the beans, it's you, Billy.*

My gaze traveled to the distant hills, and I knew I had to ask. "Gram, I've got questions."

Both of us stared into the thick trees beyond Gram's clearing. "I need to know about Mr. Satan."

Gram let out a deep breath. "You ain't gonna let it go, are you, Billy James?"

A thread of purpose wove itself through me. "No, ma'am."

Her gaze held me, but it wasn't the dark look that usually made me sweat. It was full of knowing, and resignation, and maybe even pride. "There's so much of your great-grandpa in you, sometimes it's as if I woke up four years old again." After a second, Gram cackled. "Hard to imagine me knee-high and wrinkle-free, ain't it?"

I pointed to my chest. "Hard to imagine *me* all grown up with a family."

Gram's expression sobered. "Not for me." She looked out over the mountain again. "Not for me."

She started to swing gentle-like, and we rocked in silence, the damp brushing at us. "We've talked a spell about knacks before. How your great-grandpa had a fixin' knack, like you. Was a time when it was more the rule than the exception, havin' a knack."

"What kinds of knacks did people have?" I asked, knowing Gram was feeling her way around to answering my question.

"Predictin' weather, for one, or finding water. Water witchers, they used to call 'em. Other knacks, like knowin' how to heal, or being able to smooth over hurt feelin's, were some our women could claim. It was just how the Almighty saw fit to bless us."

"But it's not like that now," I said. My pulse thrummed heavy and low as I thought about Preacher Cal's sermon about the wrongs of witchcraft, soothsayers, and fortune tellers.

"The world moves on, with or without folks," Gram said, pushing a hank of hair behind her ear. "Kelseyville started to move on when we got us a new preacher after our longtime godly soul passed on. This new preacher had some fixed ideas 'bout what was pleasin' in God's eye and what wasn't. Knacks weren't, 'cording to him." She frowned. "He convinced a few, who convinced more, that our ways went against God's law."

Gram stood, her knees creaking. "Come on, boy." She started down the steps. "Walk with me."

"Why'd people listen to him?" I asked as we headed toward scrub near the edge of her clearing.

"Facts were, that year was tough. Drought in the summer, followed by a freezin', bone-breakin' winter. There were babies that died. People went hungry. What little would grow up in the hills didn't fare well." Gram pushed a tangled vine of redbud out of our path. "Darned if that didn't bear out the preacher's words."

Gram stopped and puffed out her chest. Her voice boomed: "Leave behind the land that's shackled you to evilness. Be like the lambs of God, my children. Turn thy back on thy wickedness, and anyone who trucks with thy devil's ways, and ye shall be saved."

My mouth fell open. She sounded like Preacher Cal! Which is when it occurred to me . . . *could that godly man have been Preacher Cal's granddaddy?*

Gram chuckled, drawing my thoughts away from things that should have been obvious. "Most heeded them words. 'Cept your great-grandpa John together with your granddaddy's family and a few others. And even though I was only a tyke, I remember the way my parents grieved for a way of life they knew was slippin' away. Wasn't nothin' gonna make my daddy leave this mountain. It had served him, and his daddy, and his daddy before him. Not that things were ever easy, but we did all right."

She gave me a sad smile and stopped in front of a gnarly old oak with scrub so thick 'round its base, you couldn't tell where the ground stopped and the tree started.

"What do you see, Billy?" Gram asked, eyes fastened on that tree.

"An old scrub oak."

"Pretty hard on the eye?"

I started to nod, then stopped. "Well, it's not trimmed all neat, but it looks cool in a wild, natural way. Like everything on the hills."

Gram smiled, eyes crinkling. "That's my boy." She got down on her knees and started yanking away handfuls of scrub from around the flaking trunk.

"Gram, what are you—" She waved me back and kept at it. Her breath rasped out in little huffs.

After a moment, she sat back. "Come here, Billy James."

I squatted beside her.

Her efforts had uncovered a stone marker at the base of the tree.

The block of quartz-riddled granite was rich and glossy from the damp. I ran a finger over the chiseled script.

The lettering was weathered but still legible. I read:

> *Here lies Stuart land*
> *Cleared and worked by Stuart hands*
> *Cain't say we tamed it, for wild it be*
> *Strong in spirit like us and free*

*Here we will stay*
*Never to be driven away*
*For our thoughts, prayers, or deeds.*
*Gavin Stuart—1842*

Pride flowed across Gram's weathered face. "Your great-great-*great*-granddaddy. Gavin came to Missouri from Tennessee with his young bride, Lenore. And his father before him came 'cross the seas from Scotland." She opened her arms wide. "This is where they settled with like-minded Scots and some Welsh. Men and women who honored the old ways and a person's right to live as they saw fit."

"But that preacher changed things," I said.

"Oh, wasn't just the preacher," Gram said, waving a hand. "Wouldn't be fair to lay it all at his sorry feet. People were fallin' on hard times and lookin' for somethin' or someone to blame, so's they could have hope that things would get better."

Why hadn't I heard all this years ago? Looking at Gram's face, I understood that to her it was still a sore wound. As a flush of heat filled me, I felt closer to the truth about Kelseyville than ever before.

"Gram, what about Mr. Satan?"

She straightened and looked over at Satan's hill. "Josef's family came 'bout forty years after most had moved down." She shook her head. "'Course, there were plenty who were keen to have a buyer for their land. Didn't think twice 'bout sellin' that piece of hillside to Josef's daddy—till later."

My mind formed quick pictures of Satan's mother

and father arriving in Kelseyville—no friends, no family, only each other and a rocky hill to call home. It must have been hard for them. Kelseyville wasn't great at welcoming outsiders.

"Come on," Gram said, brushing off dirty palms. "I need to get down the hill and start supper for you boys."

We walked to the truck, my thoughts wrapped around Gram's words, but there was more I needed to know. "But why does everyone think the bad stuff that's happened to us and Gloria was Satan's doing?"

Gram's hand froze above the truck door handle. She turned and looked at me with a narrow gaze. "Who's been sayin' that?"

"Preacher Cal, for one," I mumbled.

After a deep sigh, Gram opened the door and slipped inside. "Get on in."

I did. The engine chugged and sputtered to life. After letting it idle for a moment, Gram angled the old Ford out onto the narrow roadway, her face rigid as stone. "That's pure nonsense, Billy. Doesn't make it less true to Preacher Cal and those like him, though."

"That's just it," I said. "No one's ever said *why* they feel that way."

Silence stretched between us, and I thought on all the things Satan seemed to know ahead of time. Chills pricked me. "Is Satan some kind of . . . witch?"

Gram grunted. "Josef ain't no witch. He's got a knowin' knack, Billy James. There's little rhyme or reason to it, but it's a powerful one in those that have it."

*A knowing knack.*

My fingers gripped the edge of the bucket seat and something unfurled inside me, like a sail catching the wind. A knowin' knack. That's why it seemed so natural. He wasn't a witch. Or under some kind of devilish influence. He had a knack. Like my fixin' knack. Like Gram's knack of plain speaking. Like Mama's cookin' knack.

"I told you what I did, Billy James, so you'd be more likely to understand how Josef's knack could inspire such strong emotion."

"But it's unreasonable," I said, my chest aching, "to shun a man for things that happened over seventy years ago that he didn't have anything to do with."

Gram was powerful quiet, and I knew she hadn't told me everything. There was more.

"People by and large tolerated Josef's knack as long as he stayed away from them, but 'course, keepin' certain fools away from *him* was another story."

She flicked on the wipers and took her time working that clutch as we jounced down the mountain. "There was a group of boys that were always ridin' Josef hard—cruel like boys can be when there's no one to make them behave better."

I thought of Ray, Tray, and Beavis.

"Josef came into town one day—guess he was 'bout six years or so older than you—to pick up supplies for his poor mama, who had suffered a stroke."

*A stroke.*

Satan's face. The crookedness of his body and hands. The episode he had in his cabin.

"—and them fool boys took after him like hounds to a lame rabbit."

*How could I have been so stupid?*

"Billy, you all right?"

I stared at Gram. "Did Mr. Satan suffer a stroke, too?"

Gram lifted an eyebrow. "Those types of things tend to get passed down in a family." She cleared her throat. "As I was sayin', the boys took after Josef. There was plenty who'd seen 'em, but none righteous enough to beat 'em back like the dogs they were."

I could see the scene filling Gram's mind, and quick pictures formed in my own. A sunny Kelseyville day. The green of the grass. The rich shades of hillside color and a cool breeze. And Satan . . . running. Trying to get back up his hill with a pack of red-faced porch hounds hot on his tail.

"What'd they do?" I asked, almost afraid to know.

"Knocked him clean off his feet and scattered his supplies. Ruined most. But remember, they was still a'feared of what they thought Josef could do, so they did it all without touching him directly. Cruel things were said, too, and there's times when words are more powerful than fists.

"Josef had had about enough, and I imagine he figured the easiest way to get them to leave be was to scare the bejesus out of 'em." Gram clucked her tongue. "'Cording to what was told to me, he reached out and grabbed the boy nearest with those long fingers, rolled his eyes up in the back of his head, and told the boy that the river would rise up and seek revenge on him and his family for their cruel deeds. It's my guess he just wanted to sound dramatic and frightening." Gram slowed the truck into first. "Which would have been fine, had what he said not come to pass."

Dread lay like a stone in my chest. "What happened?"

"The boy drowned in the river six days later. Dived in and never came back up. They didn't find his body, either, which near made his family crazy with grief. And his brother, who'd been with him when it happened, was never the same. Hated Josef with a passion that bordered on obsession, and fired up most of the town to feel the same. Whether it was actually his knowin' knack rearing its head or just coincidence, who can say, but it was after that that Josef's daddy sent him away to live with relations overseas."

Silence stretched between us as I contemplated Gram's revelation. The town's hatred of Mr. Satan made sense now, in a sad, twisted way. Didn't make it right, but I could understand how those types of feelings could fester and grow.

"But Mr. Satan came back," I said.

Gram nodded. "Came back for his mama's funeral. His daddy died not long after, and Josef's been here ever since."

I stared out the foggy window. "All that time living alone up on the hill . . . no friends. no family." A dull ache filled me. I couldn't imagine that kind of life. "So the town hates Mr. Satan because everyone thinks he cursed some kid to his death all those years ago?"

With a sigh, Gram switched off her wipers and brought the truck to a stop. "There's an old saying, Billy James: A prophet is never welcome in his own backyard." She shook her head, hair escaping its knot. "Most don't really hate him. They're fearful. Scared of facin' the truth about their own narrow-mindedness."

Both of us looked out the windshield toward Satan's mountain.

Which is when I spotted the smoke.

The clouds were heavy, but it wasn't mist climbing the rocky hillside. Ominous billows of heavy white smoke rose in a pillar from the side of the mountain.

*Satan.*

I was out the door like a shot. Gram's voice crying out, "Lord, oh, Lord, what have they done?" trailed me as I ran.

As the wind whipped into my eyes, I prayed like I'd never done before.

*Don't let them have hurt him, God.*

*Please . . . God . . . please. . . .*

# CHAPTER 23

I panted something fierce as I struggled up Satan's hill, pushed my way through the scrub, around trees, and straight into—

Our foreheads met with a *thud,* laying us both out on the needle-strewn forest floor.

For a moment, only our heavy breathing filled the air.

Hog.

"Gn-gnat."

I sat up, rubbing my temple. "What are you doing here, Hog?"

His eyes darted left and right, and his mouth worked like a trout on dry land. "I—well, I had to see if they really d-did it. If—" He ran a shaking hand across his face and stood. "Darn, Billy. They really did it."

My body went cold and my throat squeezed tight-closed. I stood on wobbly legs and started back up the hill toward Satan's cabin.

Hog scrabbled beside me, words falling out of his mouth one right after the other.

"—didn't think they'd really do it, you know?"

"—no one even showed up to put it out."

"—you spend time with him, Gnat? Like Sue Anne said?"

Hog grabbed my arm and pulled me to stop. We faced each other. "Gnat! You gonna answer me?"

I yanked my arm away. Maybe Hog was more like his daddy than I'd thought. As we stared at each other, I couldn't help but notice the dread in his eyes, and I realized Hog didn't know any better.

Up until three weeks ago, neither did I.

I'd been just as guilty—following everyone's lead in their hate and fear of Satan.

Without answering Hog, I pushed past him and kept on going.

I cleared the rise and stepped into the glade. There were no birds. No buzzing insects. No gentle swish and sway of pines. It was still as death.

My gaze riveted in slow motion on the smoking shell that was once Satan's cabin. Only black jagged logs and the granite foundation remained. I turned to the shed and paddock. It was gone, too. Pieces of wood too damp to burn speared upward like charred fingers, as trails of white smoke drifted away on the breeze.

And with that breeze came the strong odor of gasoline.

My stomach lurched. Buzzing—in my head, like so many bees trapped inside my skull. I stumbled forward. My toe connected with something hard. I knelt, and came up with Satan's fox. The one he'd been carving that afternoon we whittled together.

I held the fox to my chest. *Where is Satan?* Surely they didn't—There's no way they would have—

My gaze scanned the smoke-filled clearing and stopped on the cabin again. If Satan had been inside . . .

Taking a deep, shuddering breath, I went to my knees. *How could they have done this?* Images of Gloria's funeral came back to me. Then Gram's weather- and age-lined face. How long till it was her time?

I moaned.

*Get up, Billy.*

Mama's pale, sickly face . . .

My fingers dug into the damp sod. "He can't be dead. He can't be."

*Get up, Billy.*

Gloria's voice, or maybe my own, cut through the panic and I staggered to my feet. The hillside was a wreck. Even the garden had been torn to bits. Everything, from new seedlings to over-wintered herbs, had been ripped up and scattered every which way. I took in a deep breath and tried to quell my horror. So, they'd done it. I couldn't change it, so what *could* I do?

*Find Satan.*

He might be hurt, or worse. I'd do whatever I could. I wouldn't run away like Hog.

While forcing my feet toward the cabin, I realized that I was sending pleas to an Almighty I swore paid me no never mind. But I couldn't seem to help myself.

My breath barely coming, I stopped at the bottom of the steps. "Mr. Satan!" I called, my voice cracking. No answer. Nothing but a tired breeze, thick with smoke and ozone. I shuffled up two steps, then three, and stopped where the porch had collapsed, showing the dark crawl space beneath charred timbers. Only hints of walls remained. No bed. No table or chairs.

"He's gone," I whispered, my mind thick and slow with anguish. "No one could have survived that."

An electric tingle shot across the back of my neck and I spun.

*Satan.*

He walked out of the forest with Penny on a lead, Gertie and Gustav trailing hesitantly behind.

I cried out and ran across the clearing, only stopping when I could wrap my arms around Satan's skinny waist. His hand rested lightly on the top of my head, and it was all I could do to not blubber like a baby.

"I am fine, Billy," he said softly.

Releasing him, I stepped back, emotion near to choking me. I scanned his face. It was gray, drawn, but very much alive. Not burned. Not scarred.

"Are you hurt?"

He shook his head and pressed a hand to his heart. "Here I am hurt." He gazed at his nonexistent cabin, and I understood.

"No," he said, as if I'd spoken the words aloud. "It is not the loss of the cabin that pains me. It is my own weakness."

"I had thought—" I looked at my feet and swallowed.

Satan sighed and drew me over to a short elm where he'd tied Penny. "When they came, I hid in the woods. They called to me, but their tone was not of reason." Satan's normally soft blue eyes hardened as they fixed on the smoldering remains of his cabin.

I rubbed Penny's nose, nausea leaving me dizzy. Remembering Hog, I scanned the woods, but he was gone. Probably on his way back to town to warn them about me being with Satan.

Well, let him. Let them come back. My hands knotted into fists, and I felt that rage building—the rage that made me snatch the table leg and take it to Ray.

Satan's warm hand on my arm broke the spell. I let out a breath and loosened my fists. He smiled his crooked smile, and I wondered how he could do it. There was no reason to smile. No reason to feel anything but pure rage.

Then it hit me.

"The wall!" I ran across the clearing, jumping a charred log and skirting the smoldering cabin, to look over the edge of Satan's knoll. Cool relief washed through me.

It was still standing. They hadn't touched it.

"They did not know it was there," Satan said from behind, having followed me over. "Did not realize we had built it."

Tears pricked and I was quick to wipe them away with the back of my hand. "I'm sorry. All those carvings in your house. All your stuff."

The thought left me breathless with loss. His animals: the wolf, bear, the girl. Realizing I was still clutching the fox, I stepped back and held out my hand.

"I—I found this out front."

Satan took the carving and closed his eyes. "I have been running, like the fox. From people. From life. Hiding on my mountain."

"I don't think it's just you," I whispered, staring at the bushes where Hog had disappeared. I thought about

Mama not getting the help she needed and sending back Mr. Porter's letters. And my daddy up and leaving. And Ray always taking off with his friends.

And me. I'd been runnin' and hidin' forever. From Mama and Ray. From Gloria. From the truth about Kelseyville.

From God.

My gaze trailed Satan's burned-out cabin and kept on going down the hillside and into the valley below. I wondered how Satan could ever fit into a puzzle of a town that only had room for pieces with comfortable edges.

"It is time to stop running."

I looked up. Resolve etched the narrow planes of Satan's face.

He pushed his hat down onto his head. "Now that I have nothing and nowhere to run to."

Dread dropped into my stomach like a rock heaved into a well. He couldn't face those that had done it. Not now. Maybe not ever. Remembering Gram's words, I placed a hand on Satan's arm. "It was fear that drove them to do it."

Satan nodded. "Fear is a powerful thing. Stronger than love sometimes."

I'd never thought of it that way. But he was right. I'm sure my daddy must have loved us. But his fear out-weighed that love, and he wasn't to have a second chance. Mama loved me, but it didn't stop her from turning a blind eye to Ray's antics. Even Ray loved me in his own way, but most of the time he was selfish and out of control.

And Preacher Cal and the others . . . they were good folks, yet fear and mistrust drove them to burn down a man's home.

*Where is the sense in that?*

I felt Satan shift and I looked up. He pulled something out of his pocket.

*My raven.*

Covered in soot, the bird was true black now, its face as bold and crafty as the day I laid knife to wood. He placed it in my hand and curled his fingers around mine.

"I cannot hide any longer." He took a deep breath and started down off his mountain.

# CHAPTER 24

My heart knocked into my throat as we trudged off the rain-slick mountain and onto the path to town. A steady drizzle had started again. Water sluiced off the brim of Satan's hat and splattered into the growing puddles on the crushed limestone of the road. I kept hold of Penny's lead rope and scurried behind.

I worried my lower lip and tried to think of something to say. Something meaningful. Something that would turn Satan from his chosen path. More harm than good could come from Satan confronting those that lit the blaze.

I squeezed Penny's lead so hard my palms burned.

*Say something, Billy.*

My gaze flicked to Satan's resolute expression, and my stomach soured. "Uh . . . Mr. Satan? Do you think it's such a good idea to go into town right now?"

Satan didn't turn. In fact, he didn't answer me at all. Just kept going, his long legs gobbling up the distance between rural Kelseyville and the neat rows of chimneys belching white smoke into the gray sky only half a mile ahead.

We kept walking. Past my house. Past Culloden Crick, which was running so fast it was more like a small river now than a weary spring. Beyond the water tower with the rickety oak ticking against the tin. Past the cemetery where Gloria lay.

I stopped as we crested the hill near the cemetery gates. Water dripped down the collar of my shirt and into my jeans.

Gloria's small, slanted writing filled my mind: *"He'll probably blame himself for whatever happens to me. . . ."*

"Do you blame yourself?" I heard myself say, the words sounding dull and hollow in the damp air, my thoughts tripping over pictures of Mama, Ms. Russell, and the carving in Satan's cabin.

Satan stopped. Water snapped off the ends of his leather coat.

"Do you think it's somehow your fault?"

I had only to look at him to know the truth. Hurt flared across the weathered planes of his cheeks and brow.

My throat tightened. "It wasn't your fault that you didn't know. She hid it from everyone. She was good at hiding things." In two strides, I was at the gate. I gripped the cold iron. "I didn't even know she had a little brother. All these years." Mist swirled at the feet of the elms and headstones, making everything look timeless . . . far away.

Satan walked up beside me.

*I want you to talk to Satan. . . . Make sure he realizes how important the time I spent with him was. . . .*

"She—she wanted you to know how important the

time you spent with her was." I gazed up into Satan's grief-stricken face. "I saw the raven you carved for her."

His eyes widened, then closed, his lips trembling ever so slightly. "The raven," Satan whispered. "A certain harbinger of change."

Satan opened his blue eyes, and I saw something beyond sorrow in them. Something akin to a deep knowledge that couldn't be beaten out or shook off. It rested in the very seat of his soul, as Gram would say. "I should have known sooner."

"It probably wouldn't have mattered," I said softly. "The doctors said she had a tangle of leaky blood vessels in her brain. They'd been there for some time, I guess, maybe even from birth."

He wiped a hand across his eyes, and his body shuddered at my words. "I miss her," I whispered. "Every day. Like nothing else ever in my life."

Satan's hand rested on my shoulder, and the reassuring weight kept my raw pain from leaking out. I leaned into his long side, and he wrapped his arm around my shoulder. We stood there, staring at the rain-soaked hillside, thinking about a freckle-faced girl with a crooked grin and a fierce spirit.

A girl that even though she was gone maneuvered us with just her memory and a few true words.

"Don't go into town," I said quietly, shivering. "Please. Don't do it."

Satan shrugged out of his coat and wrapped it around my shoulders. It covered me from shoulder to ankle and pooled in the mud at my feet. He knelt, his blue eyes rimmed with pain. "I don't have anywhere else to go. There, at least, is a hotel, and a place to board the animals."

A quick idea filled me. "They can stay in our barn. Cammy won't mind. And you . . . you can stay—"

"With me."

Satan and I looked up. We'd been so intent on our misery, neither of us had heard Gram. She'd parked the truck at the bottom of the rise and walked up.

Rain rolled off her scarf-covered head and her dark eyes sparkled even in the dim light. "It's near dusk, and these critters need to get out of the rain." She nodded at us. "Along with you two no-sense boys."

Satan stood, and I could tell by the uncertain look on his face that he was reluctant to involve Gram and me in his troubles. He opened his mouth, but Gram raised a hand. "I won't hear an argument, Josef Satan. Never would I be able to face your mama and daddy at the pearly gates were I to turn you out in a time of need." Gram rubbed the small of her back. "And if you hadn't noticed, I'll be at those gates sooner as opposed to later, 'specially if I don't get out of this damp." She turned and headed for the truck.

We followed her down and stopped at the truck. Gram nodded at me. "Billy James, you take those critters on to your barn, and I'll take Josef to the cabin."

"They'll be okay," I said, looking at Mr. Satan. "I'll take good care of them."

"Of that I have no doubt, Mr. Wilkins."

"Mr. Wilkins? I thought I'd graduated to Billy," I said.

Satan inclined his head, a ghost of a smile on his angular face.

Gram started the truck and gave me a firm look. "You stay home now, hear?"

I nodded, a sick feeling in my gut. How would I ever be able to face Preacher Cal or Mr. Williams again? Or even Hog?

Gram's truck sputtered and jerked up the roadway, and I turned toward the town I'd called home my whole life. In the gray of dusk, it looked different—exposed. I used to think of Kelseyville as a bright place, full of color and familiar smiling faces. Rich, springtime scents and warm cocoa on a cold winter day. Free candy from Mr. Wallace at Kelley's Drug and affectionate pats on the head.

The images I had of Kelseyville were like wrapping paper on a gift. All shiny and special. But eventually you had to unwrap the gift and see what the package held. Might be that special comic book or an all-day pass to Water World in Branson. Or it might be five tantalizing flavors of imported German mustard.

I felt like I'd finally unwrapped Kelseyville and got mustard. I knew Kelseyville wasn't perfect. That it had its lumps. I'd just never bothered to consider how those lumps might affect me.

Unlike Gloria. She had been trying to rip off that wrapper for as long as I can remember. And we just kept burying her under more paper, more ribbon, more senselessness.

I was right. Cammy didn't care one way or another that she had boarders. After a wet sniff, she went right back to chewing on her alfalfa. I rubbed Penny down and gave her and the goats some feed, then turned off the light and headed for the house.

Ray was home, and my heart thumped fast against my rib cage. Would he know anything about the burning? I didn't think he had a hand in it, but there was a time not long ago when I'd suspected him of worse.

With my hand wrapped around the raven in my pocket, I went inside. Amazingly, the lights were on, and Ray was at the kitchen table staring at me.

I closed the door and tried to swallow past the lump in my throat. "What's wrong?" I said. "Is it Mama?"

Ray leaned back, his legs locked at the ankle beside the table. "Mama's fine. The hospital called earlier. They took her off the machine and she's been awake off and on."

The knot in my chest loosened—just a bit. "That's great. We've got to go see her—"

Ray cleared his throat and my thoughts stopped cold. "We had visitors. Lookin' for you."

The back of my neck tingled. *They came to my house?* "Preacher Cal?"

Ray nodded. "And a few others. I told them you wasn't home, and they started grilling me about where you were, and if I knew where you've been spendin' all your time."

I held my breath.

"Seems as if you and me were supposed to have been building some type of planter for Mama, 'cording to Mr. Williams."

I opened my mouth, then closed it. I wasn't going to lie. Not now. What was the point? "I told him that," I said softly.

Ray nodded and tapped his fingers on the table. "I asked him, what was it to him? They started givin' me attitude, so I showed them the door. Don't no one come into my house and give me attitude."

So *that's* why they hadn't known about the wall. Ray hadn't ratted me out, and Mr. Williams never figured a skinny little boy and a crippled man could build a wall.

"You gonna tell me what's going on, Gnat? Or do I have to beat it out of you?" Ray asked quietly.

My eyes cut back to Ray. I took a deep breath and told him, starting as near the beginning as I could and moving forward from there. I left out a lot, but I did tell him about Satan's cabin getting burned down and Gram taking him in. I wasn't sure how Ray'd react. He didn't have good feelings about Satan, just like everyone else in town. Not that he understood any better than I did, till recently, why he felt that way.

Ray whistled low 'tween his teeth. "You attract freaks near as easy as a flat rock does worms." He shook his head. "Mama's gonna have your hide when she gets home."

"Most likely," I said with a sigh.

Ray stood, took up his truck keys, then grabbed his hat off the rack by the door and smashed it onto his head. "I'm goin' out now that you're home. You stay put in case the hospital calls about Mama." He fixed me with a firm glare. "And you let Gram deal with that mountain freak. Got it?"

I nodded, not up to an argument and suddenly so bone weary, it was all I could do to take myself upstairs to bed.

# CHAPTER 25

Mama's heart was getting stronger every day, and part of me felt it was God's way of giving me a bit of hope. A way of saying, "Things *can* get better, Billy. I haven't forgotten about you."

Ray'd actually driven me up twice and hung out at Mama's bedside about as long as he could stand it. Each passing day she was a little bit more like herself. She made a fuss over Ray's hand. He shrugged off Mama's concern, saying it was no big deal—an accident while helping Beavis and Tray do some yard work.

I didn't know what to make of Ray lying to make things easier on me. I guessed he figured I'd get a big enough whuppin' once Mama found out about Satan and had strength to give it. Honestly, I think it was because he didn't want to worry Mama any more than was necessary, which left me thinkin' that maybe there was hope for Ray after all.

Mama would probably be coming home outside a week, long as she kept progressing. Maybe the worst was behind us. Gram would be staying on to help, or, more truly, to muscle Mama into taking it easy. Neither Gram nor I figured Ray to hang around much once Mama was home. He was itching to be off with his posse. Back out "finding his way," as he was fond of saying.

He'd gotten his job back at the mill. Which was a good thing, 'cause with all the medical bills, Mama'd be in no position to help Ray out. The bounty hunter test would have to wait, and while I still couldn't picture Ray on the right side of the law, I figured he'd take the test as soon as his hand was healed and he could scrape up the cash.

And then there was Satan. He hadn't had much to say the past three days, just whittled nearly nonstop on Gram's front stoop. I took him all the spare scraps of wood I could find, and he kept carving out critter after woodland critter.

Before long there was a line of animals stretching from one end of Gram's porch to the other, almost as if Noah's ark was settin' to sail right there off Cane's Hill. Some were close replicas to the ones I'd seen in Satan's cabin. Others were fresh and new. Like the piebald mockingbird that lived under Gram's eaves and chattered at us morning, noon, and night. She'd even started to copy Gertie's bleat, which was unnerving, hearing that sound drifting down from the roof.

I'd managed to avoid going into town the past few days as well. My feelings were a jumble, and knowing some of the history behind the hate didn't make my outrage any less, or erase a fierce need for justice that boiled to the surface in quiet moments. I kept thinking of Mrs. Williams's wide smile and wondering if she could still smile after what they'd done. How could anyone in town feel good about themselves? They might not all have done it, but weren't they always going on about helping their neighbors and taking care of their own?

My gaze strayed once more to Satan's bent head. Wasn't a single one of them that took care of Mr. Satan.

Seeing him there, doing what he'd been doing for the past week, I itched to know what his plans were. Would he rebuild? Go overseas to those relatives in Bulgaria or the Czech Republic? As we sat on the porch in the late afternoon, him carving a fierce-looking tom and me whittling on a new project—an old hound dog—I knew it was time to ask.

My question wasn't halfway out before Satan's hands stilled and his shoulders tensed. "I do not want to leave," he said quietly. "But I do not see an alternative—yet. I have spent all this time thinking . . . praying for a solution." Satan leaned back on the porch and let out a deep breath. "And whittling, hoping something will come to me in these moments of meditation, but as of yet, the answer has eluded me."

"Why can't you just rebuild?" I asked, then just as quickly bit my lip in shame. How would Satan do that? He had no supplies. For a home we needed lots of concrete. Stone. Good, pressure-treated lumber.

And most important, more hands.

Satan bent back to his wildcat and I looked at my half-formed hound in frustration. I turned the floppy-eared pooch over, memories of Sunshine, our old tick hound, filling my mind. She was as sweet as Mama's cinnamon rolls, soft and loving. Unless she had a reason not to be. When Sunshine felt someone needed to take notice, she'd bark her fool head off till we listened.

The wood felt warm under my hand. My eyes rested on Satan, head bowed, wood wedged in the crook of one hand as he worked—and an idea came to me.

Quick as lightning, I shaped up the rest of Sunshine, her big, deep eyes and her long, whippin' tail. Taking a few deft chunks, I finished her braying mouth and held her up. It was Sunshine, all right. I grinned, stuffed her into my pocket next to the raven, and stood.

"I'll see you later, Mr. Satan. I've got some toasters to fix."

Satan barely looked up, just nodded, and I headed down Gram's hill.

With my heart thumping hard, I walked into town, backpack slung over my shoulder.

My first stop was Mrs. Fitzsimmons. "Why, Billy James. I'd thought you'd grow'd up and moved on to college, it's been so long since I've seen you."

"No, ma'am. Just been busy helpin' a friend. But I brought your toasters."

Inside her kitchen I pulled out the toasters I'd fixed and put them on her counter, making sure she knew exactly where they were.

"You are such a good boy, Billy James." She shuffled over to her coffee table, pinched a butterscotch out of a bowl, and placed it in my hand. "How 'bout stayin' a spell?" Her toothless grin was wide, and I grinned back.

"Mrs. Fitzsimmons," I said as we sat on her old hide sofa. "I've got a story I'd like to tell you."

She clapped her hands, her glasses jiggling on her nose. "Oh, good! I just love stories. Is it one I've heard before, do you think?"

For a moment my breath caught and I wondered if I was doing the right thing. Then my hand closed around Sunshine. I cleared my throat and went on. "I don't think so. This one's a true story about a man that lives hereabouts who's in dire need of some help." With her attention fixed on my every word, I told her about Satan. I never said his name, just talked about what kind of man he was. What his life had been like. What wonderful things he could do with his hands. And finally how his house had burned to the ground. All his belongings. All his carvings.

Mrs. Fitzsimmons pressed a hand to her chest. "That's just terrible, Billy James."

I opened my backpack, pulled out one of Satan's recent carvings, and placed it in her open hand. She took the buck and gasped, her fingers tracing every ridge and antler tine. "Why, Billy James, I've never seen the like. This is a godly wonder."

"Yes, it is. And so is he, which is why I'm going to be askin' people to pull together and help him rebuild," I said.

"Who is this man?" Mrs. Fitzsimmons asked, her water-blue eyes still fastened on the maple buck.

I took a deep breath and prayed. "Josef Satan," I said quietly.

Her wrinkled hand stilled, and slowly she put the carving down on the coffee table. "Josef Satan, you say?"

"Yes, ma'am."

Silence stretched between us, and I watched the river of emotion flow across her face. Uncertainty. Fear. Confusion. "And *he* did that carving?"

"He did. And he's still doing them, while he contemplates the fact he may have to leave his home. The place where his mama and daddy are buried. The mountain that raised him and still holds his heart."

"And you say his cabin burnt down?" Mrs. Fitzsimmons asked so softly I almost didn't hear.

"Yes. And his barn. And his garden torn apart."

"Sounds like a mighty storm hit his land," she said, her lip trembling.

Heat rushed to my face at the memory, and I took a deep breath. "That it did, ma'am."

After a moment, Mrs. Fitzsimmons sighed deep and placed a pale hand to her cheek. "Why does he want to stay, Billy James?" she asked. "Why is it so important to rebuild?"

Truth worked through me like Gloria's plain words. "Because it's his home, Mrs. Fitzsimmons. Just like it's ours. He belongs here, like the mountains, and the redbud, and that buck on your table."

I stood. "You need any help with that toaster, you just call, Mrs. Fitzsimmons."

Mrs. Fitzsimmons remained frozen on the couch, hands in her lap, face starin' straight ahead. The buck was still on her table, and I left it, knowing it might make the only difference between her having listened or shutting me out like a weather-sealed door.

My next stop was Mrs. Fitzsimmons's neighbor, Mrs. Batey. I left a badger with her, its prickly hair a good match for her thorny disposition, but she heard me out, only closing the door after I'd given her the watch I'd fixed for her husband.

I'd thought long and hard on those I'd speak to, and my careful planning was rewarded by each one hearing me out, even if they scoffed, or scowled, or just clammed up. None slammed the door in my face, and each of them, man or woman, was transfixed with the carvings, till I told them who'd made them. After that, they were likely to drop them straight to the floor. And if they did, I'd pick them up, set them on tables, or porch rails, or swings. But I always left one, even if they'd rather I not.

I kept going until I'd returned all the items I'd fixed in my workshop over the past few months. Then moved on to some folks I'd yet to start a project for. My initial greeting was one of how I might help them, and I'd usually come away with a clock, or watch, or some even pointed out a leaky sink. Then I'd tell them about Satan, and his great need. If they felt tricked, they never said. A greater hand than mine led me along—kept me going even when I felt it was a waste of time.

Whether or not any truly listened, I didn't know, couldn't tell. But the ones who hadn't been directly involved had to be given a chance. A chance they never gave Satan. Or Gloria.

# CHAPTER 26

'd gone up Satan's hill every day for the past four days, hoping . . . waiting. But all I ever saw was that burned-out shell, and ruined garden, and below it all, the strong wall holding everything up.

Spring break would be over in less than four days, and I'd be back at school with Hog, and everyone else who most likely knew about Mr. Satan. My stomach soured at the idea.

"Satan's got 'bout as much hope of makin' that happen as a fish does of breathin' on dry land," Ray said.

I looked up from where I was staring out the kitchen window. "What?"

Ray straightened from where he was at the fridge and popped the top of his soda. "You losin' it, Gnat? You just said, 'Satan's gotta rebuild.'"

I rubbed a hand across tired eyes. "I did?"

Ray snorted. "You really need to get a life." He walked away shaking his head, and I slipped off the bench by the window and made my way outside. The morning air was warm and full of promise. The rains had finally stopped, and the land was just beginning to dry out.

It was fishing weather. Or fort-building weather. Or deer-trackin' weather.

My eyes strayed to Gram's hill. Was Satan still there whittling like crazy on her stoop? He must have noticed his carvings had gone missing, but he never said a word. I chewed my lower lip and felt a desperate need to make a decision *for* Satan. To somehow convince him, and myself, that we could rebuild his cabin, just the two of us. Like we did the wall. Side by side.

I walked down the steps and kicked Ray's cigarette bucket aside, flinging butts and kitty litter across the yard. "Oh, heck," I muttered, kneeling to pick it up. As I rose, I caught a whiff of something. My attention fell to the bucket in my hands, but the smell wasn't stale butts and ash.

It was fresh-burning timber.

Too early in the season for a forest fire. My gaze scanned the horizon and I spotted a curl of smoke.

On Satan's hill.

Dread near choked me where I stood. *Had they gone back?* What was left to burn? His trees? The mountain itself?

I dropped the bucket and took off running.

By the time I crested Satan's rise, my breath rasped in fury as well as exhaustion. I stumbled into the clearing, a snarl on my lips.

Thick, white smoke billowed up from an enormous pile of half-charred timbers and debris. My mouth must've been hanging open. I couldn't speak. Couldn't quite believe my eyes at all.

There weren't many. A total of five or six. Mr. Batey

was there. And two other men from town. Nurse Petranski was clearing the garden, while Mrs. O'Dell wove new chicken wire around salvaged posts. My gaze flicked to Mr. Waldorf, sweatin' and puffin' as he whacked out another charred log from its foundation, then slung it into the pile that was feeding the fire.

He straightened when he spotted me and lowered his sledgehammer. Others, having noticed, turned in my direction. Powerful emotions like I'd never felt swelled inside me, but I held them in, walked over, and picked up a shovel.

I met each of their gazes, nodded in greeting, then started tossing debris onto the pyre, one shovelful after another.

The next day there were two more. Mr. Duncan and Phil Laegler. No one did much talking; we were too busy working. After the old barn and cabin had been completely demolished, they started truckin' in supplies. I wasn't sure where they bought them, as I didn't figure Mr. Williams had given his blessing to our little endeavor.

Funny, but no one said a word about Satan. Not one whisper or comment. I let it go. One step at a time, as Satan would say, focus on one task before looking toward another.

Turns out the cabin foundation was still solid, having been set with thick mountain granite all those years ago. After some discussion, Mr. Duncan and Mr. Waldorf decided to add to what was already there, formed up an addition to the foundation, and on that second day, started their pour. I don't imagine Satan's hill had seen so much activity since the days when dinosaurs roamed this part of the country.

I'd purposely avoided Satan, as a part of me was afraid of what his reaction might be. And if Gram knew anything about what was going on, she didn't say a word. Just kept Satan busy doing chores around her cabin.

Things were moving along quicker than I thought possible, as everyone worked at an almost feverish pace. I knew they wanted to be shut of the project . . . of the possibility that they'd made the wrong choice, being there. But what mattered to me was that they were there at all. Despite their fear. Despite the complications their decision might hold.

With school back in full swing, my time on the project was limited to the hours I could cram in after the last bell rang until deep dark. Thankfully, other than a few whispers and cold stares, I'd been pretty much ignored in class. It was obvious they didn't know the real story. There'd come a time when that might change, but right now I didn't have the energy to try and explain.

Besides, there were some trying to do the right thing.

On day four the walls were up, and Mr. Duncan brought in roof shingles, a set of six windows, and a solid front door. I couldn't imagine where the money for the supplies was coming from, and I knew that Mr. Satan would insist on paying each and every penny back. That had me worried, but I pushed my concern aside and focused on getting done what we could get done.

I'd started piecing together a new bench for his porch, a few chairs, and even a rough-looking coffee table. Mrs. O'Dell was already sewing curtains for the windows that we had yet to install. "I think a nice, simple floral pattern would work well, don't you, Billy?"

I looked at the swath of cotton fabric. "Yes, ma'am."

Her expression serious, she nodded, then bent back to her task. I hid a grin and went back to mine.

"Billy James Wilkins, how long do you figure to hide this from him?" asked Gram after breakfast on day five.

I chewed my lower lip and tried to avoid Gram's penetrating gaze. "Well, I wasn't exactly hiding it," I mumbled.

Gram "hmphed" and gave the counter one last wipe before taking off her apron. "Boy, you are playin' with fire here. I'm not sayin' what you're doin' isn't a good thing, the *right* thing, but he deserves to know."

Her expression softened, and she reached out a hand to tap the picture of Mama on the fridge. "Your mama will be proud of you, Billy James, and thank the Almighty she'll be home this weekend." Her eyes went firm again. "That means you need to straighten all this out before then. Let him know—today."

With that I wandered outside in the bright May sunshine, wonderin' what Satan's reaction would be.

As I walked to Gram's, it occurred to me, why tell him at all?

"I'm bringing him up," I said.

They all stopped what they were doing and stared at me with hooded eyes. "He deserves to know what you all have been doing for him."

Nervous glances flicked between neighbors and friends, and after a moment, Mr. Waldorf cleared his throat and stepped forward. "Billy James, we talked about it, and if it's all the same, we'd rather not be here when he comes. We helped with the house because it was the right thing to do after . . . after what happened. But we aren't of one mind on, uh, on . . ."

He couldn't finish. What had I expected? It didn't matter what I thought. It was what it was. I couldn't change a person's conscience or ease fears that had grown for over four decades with only a sad story and the opinion of one twelve-year-old. Two, if Gloria were still here.

"Okay," I said, looking at their tense faces. "Tomorrow night. I'll bring him up tomorrow night."

# CHAPTER 27

I spent the entire afternoon after school with Satan at Gram's. We cleaned out the chicken coop and repaired rain damage to the shed. As the sun started to make its way west, I wiped my forehead off on my shirt and told Satan I had something important to show him.

His eyebrows raised, and it was all I could do to not blurt it out right there.

"Something important?" Satan asked.

"Yes, sir." I pictured the cabin that was shaping up fine, and swallowed. "It's important."

After a nod, Satan took a long sip of water, then stood. "Let us go, then."

It was obvious where we were headed, and as we started up the road, he looked at me curiously. I kept my gaze straight and picked up the pace. Gertie and Gustav trotted ahead.

Butterflies filled my gut and sweat beaded on the back of my neck.

Like that first day I went to find Satan, we walked the deer path, the dark of the woods urging us along. We came out of the trees at the back of Satan's clearing, and stopped.

Surprise widened my eyes. They'd gotten the roof done—and the windows in, and the door on. And the garden . . . the ground was freshly tilled, the fence re-strung and gated.

My gaze cut to Satan, who stood frozen beside me. Only his eyes moved, scanning, taking it all in, slowly.

I opened my mouth, but words didn't seem right, so I took Satan's hand and led him forward instead. We stopped at the garden first. "You can replant. It's not too late in the season," I said.

We walked by the barn. It was a little larger than the original, and the attached shed, while it was missing its door, was roomy enough to put by winter stores as well as feed. And the barn had three open stalls, and some-one had even stacked several bales of hay in the corner. Satan's chickens had already taken up residence. "You could get an extra goat," I said, "or even a milk cow, if you wanted."

Satan didn't respond, just looked, so I took him onto the front porch steps. The stones were from the original cabin, but the deck was bright and shiny with its new pine slats and overhang. "The damage to the foundation wasn't so bad," I said. "They were able to save a lot."

With a gentle tug, I opened the front door and led him inside. There sat my rough table and chairs in the kitchen, which was still empty of cabinets and appli-ances, but you could see the potential. "They built on another room," I said like a Hollywood tour guide. "But come into the living room—it's larger. Not by much, but enough."

We walked under the kitchen lintel and into the main room. Someone had brought in a sofa and sat it against one wall; the other held a nice-looking bookshelf. There were no books on it . . . but there were other things.

Satan's grip tightened on my hand and we walked over together. On each shelf sat his carvings. Bear, bird, deer, and wolf. They'd been neatly lined up to face outward, each individual expression speaking volumes about the man who had made them.

Satan released my hand and reached, his fingers trembling. He picked up the buck I'd given Mrs. Fitzsimmons. "The message. I did not believe it," he whispered. Our eyes met, and I saw awe in Satan's blue gaze. "All those days, carving. The only answer I received was patience. Like the buck as he waits for the spring grass to reappear." Satan set down the buck and picked up the bear. "And the bear when he hibernates—waiting—knowing his time to reemerge will come."

He looked so pale, I eased Satan over to the couch, and we both sat.

"Billy, my faith was weak." He opened his jacket, pulled something out of his pocket, and handed it to me.

I opened the paper jacket and scanned the slip. A ticket. A bus ticket to St. Louis. My breath stopped. He was planning on leaving. I checked the date: Monday. Tomorrow.

"You can't leave," I said quickly. Gloria's face eased into my mind and I grabbed at her image like a drowning man to a chunk of wood. "Gloria would want you to stay."

We sat in silence. Crickets started to chirp, and dusk filled the corners of the room with shadows.

He sighed and stood. "I will not decide tonight. Not here. There is much to think on."

There were a million things I wanted to say, remind him of. His parents' graves. Gertie and Gustav, and Penny.

*And you, Billy, don't forget yourself. . . .*

I jerked in surprise at Gloria's voice so clear in my head. A chill crept up my spine as I followed Satan outside. It wasn't my place to tell Satan what to do. Not after all Kelseyville had done to him—and willing or not, I'd been a small part of it.

We stopped at the edge of Mr. Satan's clearing and he looked up into the darkening sky. I joined him, head tipped back. Stars were just starting to appear, and the heavens felt closer than ever before.

"This is God's land, Billy James Wilkins," Satan said softly. "Don't let anyone cause you to think differently."

# CHAPTER 28

Morning came so fast I didn't figure I had slept at all. Before dawn had broken all the way across the sky, I dressed for school and was on my way to Gram's. She was on her porch swingin' when I jogged up, my breath coming fast.

"Satan—is he . . ."

Gram inclined her head. "Went walkin'."

I looked in the direction her head tipped, my forehead scrunched in consternation. He could have gone anywhere. Into town, the graveyard, or even his hill. "Gram, didn't he say?"

She shook her head. "I'm not his mama that he needs to tell me where he's goin'."

I took off in the direction she'd indicated. There was only an hour before school. I stopped at Gloria's grave site first. No Satan. I touched her headstone, which had been put in place sometime in the last few days. "I'll find him, Gloria. Don't you worry."

My next stop was the bus station in town, but the small bench outside the drugstore was empty. I ran up and down a few of the side streets, but Satan was nowhere to be found.

That left only one place.

I took the familiar path to Satan's newly built cabin. I ran to the house first, knocked, then went inside. He wasn't there. Next I hit the barn and shed.

No Satan.

Could he have already left? The thought made me ache so deep I had to sit right there on the barn's dusty floor. My hand went automatically to the raven in my pocket, and I took a deep breath. "Satan, where are you?"

A soft bleat broke the stillness, and I scrambled to my feet. I stood and listened, praying.

*"Nahhhhh . . ."*

With determined steps, I walked into the woods and around to the side of Satan's knob. I found him standing, staring at our wall, Gertie and Gustav yanking leaves off nearby trees.

Tingling erupted up through my feet and into my calves as I strode over. Standing beside him, I looked at what we'd built. It had weathered a bit in the past days, but in a good way. Making it look a part of the hillside. As if it had always been there.

"We did well with this, Billy," Satan said quietly, the breeze teasing hair across his scalp.

"Yes, sir," I replied. "It will stand longer, I think, than the short time you said it might."

Satan's gaze left the wall and fell on my face. His bright blue eyes stared straight into mine and he smiled. "I believe you are right. It just might."

Mama came home the following Saturday to a spotless house, a kitchen full of home-cooked meals, and three attentive nursemaids. That lasted all of an hour before Mama demanded we stop hovering over her like flies on cheesecake.

Her voice filled the house:

"Mama Hester, you've done enough 'round here to put me to shame!"

"Raymond Clay, why aren't you at work?"

"Billy James, go find a friend to soak up some of this soul-warmin' springtime with."

Didn't take Ray more than a second to light out once he had been officially relieved of his duty.

I trailed Ray outside.

He checked his radiator, then shot a glance my way. "Whatcha want, Gnat?"

"You still planning on taking that test once your hand's better?"

His lips thinned, and he shrugged. "Haven't decided yet. What's it to you?"

I copied his shrug, my toes scuffing dirt. "Well, I've been thinking. I have a little bit of money from helping Mr. Satan build that wall. I could, like, lend you some, if you want."

Ray stared at me hard, and it was impossible to read from his expression what he was thinking.

He went back to wiping his windshield clean. "No thanks. 'Sides, you might need it to help Mama out with school lunches and stuff. But don't worry. . . ." Ray stuffed the rag he'd used on the windshield into his back pocket before slipping into the cab and slamming the door, a smirk on his face. "I'm not gonna ask Mama for anything. And she's got plenty socked away for you and your big 'college plans.' She'd die before she'd touch that money." He started the engine and gave me the chin flip nod before driving away.

*She'd die before she'd touch that money.*

Ray's words rang in my head and my mouth dried up as I put two and two together.

No. It couldn't be the reason Mama didn't do what the doctor said, *could it?*

I walked back into the house in a daze.

Gram was sitting in the chair near Mama's bed, her small, wrinkled hand covering Mama's thick yellow one.

Gram rose. "I'll be in the kitchen, Sarah."

And we were alone.

I stumbled in and sat. "Mama," I started, unsure how to continue.

She reached out and I took her hand. It was warm, soft. The calluses on her palm were fading back to supple flesh after three weeks of no kneading and scouring. "Billy James, Gram tells me you were a great help while I was away."

"I—I just did what I needed to do."

Her look was one of patient understanding, and for the first time in what seemed like forever, I felt comfortable in my mama's company.

She patted my cheek. "You always do, Billy James." Her gaze wandered out the window. "You've a knack for being responsible, for knowing how to fix things that aren't working."

"I don't know about that," I grumbled.

Her attention snapped back to my face, her eyes firm. "Well, I do. It's the way of it. No reason to act different. And I'm a fool for ignoring it for this long."

I had no idea what to say to *that,* so I changed the subject. "Mama, you, uh, didn't refuse to do what the doctor said 'cause you didn't want to spend money you were saving for me, right?"

Her eyebrows rose and some of her old fire crept into her voice. "Billy James, where'd you get an idea like that?"

I snapped my mouth closed and wished I had enough sense to keep it that way more often.

She held up a hand. "That oldest boy of mine needs to mind his own." Mama inclined her head. "It's true. I've been saving for your college. But money was NOT why I didn't do what Doc White told me to. Was just plain foolishness that kept me from that. Understand?" She grabbed my chin, and I was quick to see that not all her strength had drained away in that hospital bed. "Understand?" she repeated.

I nodded and she let me go. Her hand caressed my chin, then dropped back to the bed.

"Did you save for Ray, too?" I whispered.

Her eyes closed, and a grim smile tugged at the corners of her mouth. "Gram said you'd found your voice these past few weeks." Her eyes opened and they were full of pride and something else. "Having the courage to speak up is a gift, but you have to learn when to use it and when to keep to yourself." A pause . . . then, "Gram told me what played out up here while I was gone."

My chest tightened. I had known Gram would explain things, and I'd been fretting about Mama's reaction the entire time. She didn't seem mad. More like worried.

"No sense in my lecturing you over all that's gone on." She sighed. "'Sides, I'm proud of you for helping like you done. There's not many who would've. And to answer your question about Raymond Clay: That boy still has a lot of growing up to do, and if it seems like I spend a lot of time and effort trying to keep him pointed in the right direction, it's because he needs it. But what he needs wouldn't be helped any by my saving money for him."

"Like Daddy?"

She sucked in a breath. "Yes. But it wasn't my responsibility to be tamin' your daddy. It *is* my responsibility to do all I can to set Raymond Clay right."

"But when does that stop? When does Ray have to take care of himself, Mama?"

Silence. She lifted her eyes. They were hard, but resigned. "I don't know."

It was a fair answer.

Mama squeezed my hand. "Time for me to get some rest, Billy James. You do what I said and go outside on this fine day."

My eyes fell on the Bible that lay on Mama's nightstand. I realized that I'd done my fair share of praying the past few weeks. I still didn't understand *why* God let things happen as they did, but I realized most of the badness that happened wasn't on account of God not doing his job, it was on account of men and women not doing what they know is *right* with God.

I squeezed Mama's hand back before letting go and walking to the door. Maybe us Wilkinses weren't so unrepairable after all.

"Billy James."

I stopped and turned.

"You're to have a visitor next weekend."

"What? Who?" I asked.

"Your Granddaddy Porter."

The room was so quiet I could have heard a flea's thought. "What?" I said again, in complete shock. *I'd forgotten all about Micah Porter!* The letter. Had he written again?

Mama raised her eyebrows. "Needed to glue something, did you?"

I could feel my face go red as a June raspberry. "Uh, well, I—"

Mama "hmphed," then let her arms fall to her sides. "He called the hospital a few days ago. I've decided to let you spend some time with him, but you're not to ask him for anything, hear? We're not beggars, and he's not going to step in like some knight in shining armor." She took a deep breath and waved me away. "We'll see how things work with Micah Porter. You just mind what I said."

"Okay," I said, meaning it. I didn't intend to ask Micah Porter for a thing, other than stuff about my daddy. But I had a right to that.

"Mama?"

She raised her eyes.

"Thank you."

"Get on, Billy James. Daylight's burnin'."

Since Hog was at baseball practice, I gave Nick a holler on the phone and started over to his house. Things had been as strained as pasteurized apple juice between me and Hog, but that was okay. I figured his curiosity about Mr. Satan would eventually win out, and he'd want to know what I knew. Maybe even meet him.

Which was a real possibility, since Satan had decided to stay. He'd moved back into the cabin that very next day.

We'd driven into Windell after school with Gram and purchased a new bed and some other essentials. Then Satan went into Kelseyville on his own not long after to buy groceries. I wasn't with him when he did, but I heard from some of the old-timers that he was polite as an easy rain, as was most everyone he encountered while there.

I still couldn't look at Preacher Cal or Mr. Williams without seeing Satan's burned-out cabin, though. I'd heard that Preacher Cal's sermons as of late had been all about redemption and the forgiveness of our sins through Christ. Not an unusual message for Christ's Corner Chapel, but timely, in my opinion.

If God and Satan could forgive them, then eventually I figured I would, too.

It didn't take much to figure that the boy that died was Mr. Williams's brother. I read the old obituaries at the library. Seeing it in print filled me with a powerful sadness that such a tragic misunderstanding was allowed to fester all this long while. I couldn't hold Mr. Williams's hatred against him, and I knew time might not ever heal those wounds.

But it wasn't something for me to fix.

I had better things to do.

Nick wobbled to a halt in front of me. "I wore my hiking boots!" He thrust out one foot and then the other.

Sure enough, he'd exchanged his slacks for jeans, and his loafers for a brand spankin' new pair of Redwings. A bright yellow T-shirt and green backpack completed his mountain duds.

At least I'd have no problem finding him if he wandered off.

"Nice shoes," I said, reaching out and ruffling his neatly combed hair.

"Hey!" he said, raising his arms to fend me off.

I grinned and yanked on his backpack straps. "Come on. We've got some explorin' to do."

We walked to the end of the roadway, then started up a narrow path that I'd taken plenty of times. Cedar and oak, thick with new growth, feathered above our heads, letting in patches of achy-bright light.

I kept my pace mild on account of Nick's short legs, but he matched it, his face a study of concentration.

"We're going to check out a crick that was flooded from the rains. It's gone back to clear, but sometimes there's interesting things that wash down with the mud and settle at the bottom."

Nick's face lit up. "Really? What kinds of things? Gold, you think?"

"Well, I've never found none, but anything's possible."

Contemplating my words, Nick went quiet, his cheeks flushed.

We heard the water before we saw it, and as we shinnied down a small embankment to stand beside the crick, Nick's expression ebbed and flowed like the crick we were getting ready to wade into.

First surprise. Then excitement. And finally a hesitant respect.

"Take off your shoes and roll up your jeans," I said. Culloden Crick was a mellow stream that trickled its way down Gram's hillside before emptying into the river below. A perfect place for Nick to get a taste of what made the Ozarks so special.

He grudgingly shed his big-money boots and rolled his pant legs up so tight I feared he might turn his legs into blue sausages.

After a few encouraging words, he joined me, his eyes as wide as Mama's plates. It helped that the rocks were round at the bottom, so as to not dig into our feet. And the weather was just warm enough that the cool of the stream felt good instead of glacial.

"Hey," Nick said, hands gripping every rock or wisp of grass for balance. "This isn't so bad. The bottom is sort of soft." He bent low and peered through the glass-clear water. "And there's sand!"

"Well, sure. You think your desert has a corner on all the sand?" I asked, smiling.

Nick frowned, his freckles bunching. "I'm not stupid, Billy."

My face went serious. "No, you're not, Nick. Not by a long shot. You and your sister had that in common." I took in his fiery expression and mumbled under my breath, "'Mong other things."

We were quiet for a bit, then I started pointing out some stuff I figured Nick might find interesting. "These little pockets of still water," I said, taking him over to a depression off to one side of the main flow. "Full of tadpoles. See?"

Nick poked his head around my waist and gasped. "Wow! There's like hundreds, no, thousands of them!" He dipped his hand right in and gasped as the little black fatheads squiggled every which way. "And just think, they'll all be frogs." I could see his mind calculating how many hoppers that would be.

We moved on, me pointing out stuff and Nick oohing or making disgusted faces, depending on what I pulled from the pools or out from under rocks. He liked the tiger salamanders and hated the crawdads.

After a time, I took Nick to a trio of flat boulders that Gloria and I used to lounge on. Water hummed at our feet as we reclined and talked about the mountain, then Gloria, then the mountain some more.

Birds screeched overhead, and Nick and I looked up. Mockingbirds. And they were put out about something. Probably us being there, but the warm rock felt too good to contemplate moving.

"Did that guy ever carve one of those birds?" Nick asked. "They're so loud."

I pictured Satan's carvings and took a deep breath. "I think he might've. Maybe you can ask him."

Nick pulled the raven out of his pocket and held it up to the light. The bird's eyes seemed to draw a bead right on us.

"You carry that everywhere?" I asked.

Nick nodded solemnly.

I touched the twin bird in my own pocket. "That's okay. It's just the right size for carryin'."

"My mom talked about him."

My breath caught, and I stared hard at the top of Nick's head. "Who?"

"The guy that carved this." Nick turned the raven over in his hands.

"Oh, yeah?" I said, sitting up. "What'd she say?"

Nick bounced the raven across the boulder, as if it were hopping from one spot to the next. "She just said she knew him when she was younger. And that he was really good at whittling. And that he lived up in the hills."

After a minute, he shrugged. "She let me keep it. So I guess it was okay." He gazed at me, his hair getting real close to hanging in his eyes. "Did he really make this from a plain old chunk of wood?"

I nodded.

He held it inches from his face. "It looks so real," he said for the hundredth time. "Remember Gloria saying she tried to carve but stunk at it? That's how it was for me with baseball. My dad made me play, even though I was totally awful. I'm not cut out for baseball, you know? But he said—"

"It builds character," I said in my best adult voice.

Nick gasped. "Yeah! That's it! How'd you know that?"

I shrugged and tossed a pebble into the pool at our feet. "Parents have to say that. It's like an oath they take or something."

Nick frowned, and I fought a grin.

"Bet Gloria wouldn't have played stupid old baseball if she didn't want to."

I had to agree with him. I handed him a pebble and he tossed it in, counting the ripples as they broke across the shadowed surface.

Talking about Gloria didn't leave me near as sad as it used to. In fact, the more I shared with Nick, the easier it was to think of Gloria and not feel that horrible tightness in my chest.

An intense look toughened Nick's face, and he rubbed the raven hard enough to get splinters.

I stilled his hand.